GO LONG!

ALSO BY
TIKI BARBER AND RONDE BARBER

GO LONG!

Tiki Barber and Ronde Barber
with Paul Mantell

A Paula Wiseman Book
Simon & Schuster Books for Young Readers
New York London Toronto Sydney

For AJ and Chason—T. B.

For my three Roses—R. B.

To my dad, Sol Mantell, who taught me
to love reading and sports—P. M.

The authors and publisher gratefully acknowledge
Mark Lepselter for his help in making this book.

SIMON & SCHUSTER BOOKS FOR YOUNG READERS
An imprint of Simon & Schuster Children's Publishing Division
1230 Avenue of the Americas, New York, New York 10020
This book is a work of fiction. Any references to historical events, real people, or real locales are used fictitiously. Other names, characters, places, and incidents are products of the author's imagination, and any resemblance to actual events or locales or persons, living or dead, is entirely coincidental.
Copyright © 2008 by Tiki Barber and Ronde Barber
All rights reserved, including the right of reproduction in whole or in part in any form.
SIMON & SCHUSTER BOOKS FOR YOUNG READERS is a trademark of Simon & Schuster, Inc.
For information about special discounts for bulk purchases, please contact Simon & Schuster Special Sales at 1-866-506-1949 or business@simonandschuster.com.
The Simon & Schuster Speakers Bureau can bring authors to your live event. For more information or to book an event, contact the Simon & Schuster Speakers Bureau at 1-866-248-3049 or visit our website at www.simonspeakers.com.
Also available in a Simon & Schuster Books for Young Readers hardcover edition.
Book design by Laurent Linn
The text for this book is set in Melior.
Manufactured in the United States of America • 0911 OFF
First Simon & Schuster Books for Young Readers paperback edition October 2011
2 4 6 8 10 9 7 5 3
The Library of Congress has cataloged the hardcover edition as follows:
Barber, Tiki, 1975–
Go long! / Tiki and Ronde Barber with Paul Mantell.—1st ed.
p. cm.
"A Paula Wiseman book."
Summary: When Coach Spangler leaves at the start of their second year of junior high school, thirteen-year-old twins Tiki and Ronde wonder if his replacement, history teacher Mr. Wheeler, can coach the Eagles to another winning football season.
ISBN 978-1-4169-3619-0 (hc)
[1. Barber, Tiki, 1975—Fiction. 2. Barber, Ronde, 1975—Fiction. 3. Football—Fiction. 4. Twins—Fiction. 5. Brothers—Fiction.] I. Barber, Ronde, 1975– II. Mantell, Paul. III. Title.
PZ7.B23328Go 2008
[Fic]—dc22
2007045843
ISBN 978-1-4169-8573-0 (pbk)
ISBN 978-1-4424-3982-5 (eBook)

EAGLES' 8TH-GRADE ROSTER

HEAD COACHES—*"SPANKY" SPANGLER, SAM WHEELER*
DEFENSIVE COACH—*PETE PELLUGI*
OFFENSIVE COACH—*STEVE ONTKOS*

KEY PLAYERS:

QB	WR
CODY HANSEN, GRADE 9	*FRED SOULE, GRADE 9*
MANNY ALVARO, GRADE 7	*JOEY GALLAGHER, GRADE 9, HOLDER*

RB	CB
JOHN BERRA, GRADE 9	*RONDE BARBER, GRADE 8*
TIKI BARBER, GRADE 8	*ANDREW SCHULZ, GRADE 7*

OL	K
PACO RIVERA, GRADE 8	*ADAM GUNKLER, GRADE 8*

DL	MLB
SAM SCARFONE (DE), GRADE 9	*MATTHEW SCHULZ, GRADE 8*

CONFERENCE OPPONENTS:
EAST SIDE JUNIOR HIGH MOUNTAINEERS
NORTH SIDE JUNIOR HIGH ROCKETS
BLUE RIDGE JUNIOR HIGH BEARS
PULASKI JUNIOR HIGH WILDCATS
WILLIAM BYRD JUNIOR HIGH BADGERS
PATRICK HENRY JUNIOR HIGH PATRIOTS
MARTINSVILLE JUNIOR HIGH COLTS

CHAPTER ONE

THE NEW "STRAW"

"I'M BREAKIN' THIS ONE BIG-TIME, RONDE!"

Ronde Barber stared back at his identical twin as they faced each other across the line of scrimmage. "In your dreams, Tiki."

"Don't blink, or you'll miss me," Tiki shot back.

Ronde let out a big yawn, patting his mouth like he was bored. "I'm *so* scared."

Then came the "Hut! Hut!" of the quarterback, Matt Clayton, and Tiki took off like a shot. Ronde backpedaled a few steps, then turned and matched his brother stride for stride.

Ronde did not look back for the ball. He kept his focus on Tiki, waiting for him to make his move. Ronde watched his eyes, knowing they would widen just before the key moment.

Ronde had learned this trick last season. It was part of his education in how to cover wide receivers. But it sure helped when that receiver was your identical twin.

He and Tiki knew each other inside out, backward and forward. They didn't just look alike, they *thought* alike.

1

Ronde could have covered Tiki with his eyes closed.

Sure enough, ten yards downfield, Tiki's eyes widened for the briefest instant. On cue, he faked to the outside, then cut to the inside, straight across the field.

Matt Clayton had already let the ball fly, a bullet speeding toward its appointed meeting place with Tiki's chest.

But Ronde was one step ahead of them both. He cut in front of Tiki, leapt into the air, and with his outstretched fingertips, knocked away the ball!

He landed hard on the grass, but it was worth it to hear Tiki's disappointed groan.

"Oh, man! You're a pest, Ronde!"

"I try," Ronde replied, grinning as Tiki reached out a hand to help him up.

"Man, I'm glad you're on *my* team," Tiki said, shaking his head.

The boys trotted back to the line of scrimmage, where their friend and practice partner, Matt Clayton, was waiting for them.

"Awesome coverage, dude!" he told Ronde. "Did you spy on us in the huddle?"

"No way," Ronde said, still smiling. "I just *knew*."

"He finishes my sentences for me all the time," Tiki told Matt.

"No, *you're* the one who does that!" Ronde protested.

"You *both* do it," Matt said, laughing. "I've heard you. It's weird."

All three boys were wearing their old blue Hidden Valley Eagles uniforms from last season. Tiki wore number two, while Ronde had number five.

Ronde wondered if the school would retire the number nine now that, starting tomorrow, Matt, last year's *Roanoke Reporter* All-World quarterback, had graduated and was moving on to Cave Spring High School.

In Ronde's opinion, Matt deserved the honor of having his number retired. He'd broken every Hidden Valley record for passing. During the Eagles' run to the District Championship this past season, college scouts had come around to see Matt play—and the ninth-grade wonder hadn't disappointed them.

This would be their last practice together for two years, until the twins made it to high school and they were all reunited.

And starting tomorrow, for Tiki and Ronde, it was back to school—back to the Eagles for another season, this time without Matt as their leader.

"Why'd you have to go and graduate?" Ronde asked Matt. "*Now* what are we going to do for a quarterback?"

"You guys'll be fine," Matt assured them. "The Eagles are even better and deeper this year. And if you're worried about Cody Hansen, don't be. He's a great athlete, and he's got a great throwing arm. I saw him play Peewee League, back when he was in sixth grade."

"He didn't play so great last year when he was subbing for you," Tiki said.

"Don't worry," said Matt. "He just couldn't handle the pressure of coming off the bench. He wasn't prepared to be a starter, that's all. He's much better than he showed last year. You'll see."

Ronde had to admit it was true. He and Tiki had been subs last year too. And when they'd gotten their chance to play, they'd had their moments—but they'd also made bad mistakes.

This year would be different. As eighth graders and second-year men, the twins would be key starters—Tiki at halfback, Ronde at cornerback. The team would be counting on them—and Ronde was sure he and Tiki had the talent to carry the team to victory.

He just wasn't so sure about Cody.

"Trust me, it's going to be fine," Matt said as they lined up for another pass play. "I mean, just think—last year, you two guys barely played! That alone is going to make the team so much better. And remember, we won the District Championship last year. So . . . can you say 'State Champions'?"

"Man, don't jinx us," Tiki said. "It's bad enough you're gone, and we have to put up with that hot dog, Cody Hansen."

"Tiki, he's just immature," Matt said. "I was the same way in seventh grade."

"Like fun you were," Ronde said. "You were never like Cody, so don't even go there."

"True, he's got better hair."

"Dude, you never say anything bad about anybody!" Tiki complained. "Stop being so nice. Cody is a ball hog, and that's all there is to it."

"If that were all," Matt argued, "Coach Spangler wouldn't have made him the starter this year."

Ronde had to admit, there was truth in what Matt said. Coach Spangler was really smart, and he knew what he was doing with his team.

"I'm telling you," Matt assured them, "as long as Spangler's in charge, the Eagles are going to win. His teams have made the playoffs seven out of eight years since he became coach. He can get the best out of anybody."

"Even Cody?" Ronde asked.

"Even Cody," Matt said. "He's talented. He just needs to get some experience."

"And a better attitude," said Ronde, rolling his eyes.

"Man, you got that right. Cody's a head case," Tiki complained. "He thinks he's all that and a bag of chips."

"I saw him the other day in Kessler's, bragging about how we're going to dominate this year," Ronde said. "I hate to hear that stuff, you know? It's bad luck to run your mouth like that."

"Don't worry so much," Matt said. "Hey, think about *me*—I'm losing the coach who taught me everything I know!"

"Aw, man, I pity you," Tiki said, pretending to play the violin.

"I'm about to start crying," Ronde joked. "Come on, yo—let's play some football! Show me something I haven't seen, dude."

"All right, now you went and made me mad," Matt said, smacking the football between his hands. "Let's go. You're toast, Ronde."

Matt put his arm around Tiki and whispered the play into his ear. Tiki lined up, and Ronde saw the corner of his mouth curl up into a secret smile. *They're up to something tricky,* he said to himself.

"Hut! Hut-hut!" Matt dropped back as Tiki took a darting step forward.

Ronde dropped back into coverage, but Tiki was only faking a forward move. With Ronde back on his heels, Tiki stopped and turned to face Matt.

Matt tossed him a quick lateral, then raced downfield, and before Ronde could recover, Tiki threw the ball into Matt's waiting arms!

"Touchdown!" Matt yelled, spiking the ball and doing a crazy little song and dance in the end zone. "Oh, yeah— go Ma-att, it's your birthday . . ."

Ronde wasn't thrilled about being beaten on the play. But Matt's celebration was so corny, he couldn't help laughing.

Hotdogging wasn't Matt's style at all. He never got into that sort of thing, like so many other players did. When he threw a touchdown pass, Matt just raised his arms in the air and yelled "YES!"

Ronde admired that about him. Unlike some people, Matt Clayton was a class act.

"I'm hungry," Tiki said. "My stomach's talking to me. It's saying, 'Let's go get some lunch!'"

"I'm in," Matt said. "Kessler's?"

"Yeah, baby," Ronde said. "I'm up for a burger and a double-thick shake."

"Trying to bulk up?" Matt teased.

Ronde and Tiki were small for their age—at least compared to the rest of the football team. Matt, already over six feet tall, towered over them.

Someday, Ronde thought, *he'll be a star college quarterback.*

He and Tiki would be stars too—but only if they kept getting taller, bigger, and stronger. Burgers and shakes might not be health food, Ronde figured, but they were a sure bet if you wanted to gain weight.

Kessler's luncheonette was an old-fashioned soda shop that had been there for over fifty years. It was only a block from Cave Spring High School—Matt's new home.

The twins had come over here to practice with him on the high school field—even though it was also the home field of Cave Spring Junior High, one of the Eagles' main rivals.

The three friends sat on swivel chairs at the counter and made fast work of their food and shakes. They were just about done eating when the front door swung open and in walked Cody Hansen.

"Yo, gentlemen!" he called out to them, raising a hand in greeting. "What's shakin'?"

"*We* are," said Tiki, lifting up his shake to demonstrate.

"Hey, are you guys psyched for this season or what?" Cody asked, high-fiving the twins. "We're going all the way to the State finals this year, dudes." Looking at Matt and raising an eyebrow, he added, "We've upgraded at all the skill positions—like quarterback."

It was a dig at Matt, and Ronde and Tiki both knew it. Ronde winced, feeling for Matt. But he needn't have worried—Matt Clayton was not the type to take an insult lying down.

"Cody, my friend," he said, "you've got all the skills, but you've still got a lot to learn. Why don't you win a game or two for the team first, before you start shooting your mouth off?"

Cody turned away from Matt and back to Tiki and

Ronde. "Hey, you dudes want to throw it around? The field's empty."

"Uh, no thanks," said Ronde. "We just got done—"

He was going to say that they'd been practicing with Matt, but Matt interrupted him.

"That's a good idea," he said, and took one last sip from his shake, draining it to the last drop. "You guys should get used to playing together."

He clapped Ronde and Tiki on the back. "See you guys around. Say hi to Coach for me, huh?" He dropped a few dollars on the counter and left, shaking his head.

"Cody, man, why'd you have to diss Matt?" Tiki asked.

"Chill, Barber," Cody said, frowning. "Matt Clayton is ancient history. This year, I am 'the man.'"

Ronde sighed, rolling his eyes. He'd seen Cody Hansen act like this before. Cody wasn't exactly modest—and he could be totally impossible when he got going.

Maybe it was because his uncle Sven was once the backup quarterback for the Cleveland Browns, and his cousin Nels was a linebacker for Clemson. Cody had several family members who were well-known athletes, and he was always, always bragging about them.

"That's right, from now on, I am the straw that stirs the drink," Cody went on. "In the Eagles' nest, I am the Big Bird. It's all in the genes, my friends. All in the genes."

Sure, he was hotdogging it, more to be funny than

9

anything else. Just like when Matt Clayton did his little touchdown dance earlier that day. But for some reason, Ronde didn't find Cody's act the least bit funny.

"You finishing that burger?" Cody asked him.

Ronde looked down at the remains of his lunch. "No, man, I'm full," he said.

"You mind?" Cody asked. But even if Ronde had minded, it would have been too late. The rest of his burger was already stuffing Cody's left cheek. "Mmmm! Good! How 'bout you, Tiki?"

"Don't be touching my food, man," Tiki said, drawing his plate closer to him and farther away from Cody's reach. "This burger is *mine,* understand?"

"Whatever," Cody said. "Come on, let's get out on the field and toss it around."

"Not today, dude," Ronde told him. "We're tired out."

"We've been practicing all morning," Tiki added.

"With Clayton?"

They nodded.

"Forget him, will you? He's yesterday's news. *I'm* the guy you've got to work out with. This is *our* year, remember?"

Ronde couldn't argue with that. It didn't matter that he liked Matt Clayton better. Cody was the leader of their team now, for better or for worse.

Ronde just hoped it wasn't for worse.

• • •

"AAAAHHHHRRRRGGH! Put me down, Paco!"

They were all at the bus stop, clowning around while they waited for the bus to take them to their first day of classes. Paco Rivera, their old pal, was practicing his tackling techniques on Tiki and Ronde, who were much smaller than he was.

Paco released his death grip on Ronde, who collapsed to the ground. "There's got to be a penalty for crushing," he said, rubbing his sore ribs.

"Man, have you been pumping iron all summer?" Tiki asked.

"My dad's been working me out on the free weights," Paco said. "Feel that muscle." He made a muscle, and his biceps popped up about three inches.

"Whoa," said Tiki, feeling it and making a face like he was touching a cockroach. "That is just sick."

"We're gonna have a monster team this season," Paco said, grinning and nodding. "Can you spell 'undefeated'?"

"Hey, man, let's not get ahead of ourselves," Ronde warned him. "We've still got to get out on that field and prove we're the best."

"It's a done deal, brother," Paco assured him. "Did you hear that Cody Hansen went to his uncle's football camp over the summer? He throws a perfect spiral now, every time—and he can throw it fifty yards!"

11

Ronde would have bet it wasn't true—probably just Cody bragging again—but he didn't argue. The bus had arrived, and it was time to get on board for another year of school.

They rode the five miles in what seemed like five seconds. By the time they'd finished saying hello to all their bus-mates from last year, they were already there!

"Hey, you guys," Paco said as they got off the bus. "There's Coach! Let's go say hi."

Coach Steve "Spanky" Spangler was standing near the steps that led up to the school's main entrance. He was talking to Mr. Pellugi, his assistant coach, who was also a Phys Ed teacher.

It looked like they were having a pretty serious conversation. "Maybe we'd better wait till after school," Ronde said, holding Tiki and Paco back.

But Paco wasn't listening. "Yo, Coach!" he yelled, raising his hand for a high five as he approached.

Coach Spangler looked up, seeming startled. He didn't smile—just gave a little half wave and turned back to Mr. Pellugi, resuming their conversation.

"Whoa," said Paco, backing away and joining the Barbers as they headed up the stairs. "That was weird."

"They must be talking about something important," Ronde said. "I guess it just wasn't a good time to say hi."

"I guess not," said Paco, but he didn't sound convinced.

Tiki was looking back over his shoulder at the two coaches, a worried expression on his face.

Whatever it was they were talking about, Ronde thought, it definitely wasn't something happy. Coach Spangler had his hand on Mr. Pellugi's shoulder and was talking intensely.

Ronde sure hoped everything was okay. It was way too early in the season for trouble to raise its ugly head.

CHAPTER TWO

A SHOCK TO THE SYSTEM

TIKI WATCHED THE HAND OF THE CLOCK ON THE wall as it ticked off the seconds till the end of last period.

Wow, he thought, as Mr. Mills droned on and on about the Dark Ages, *a minute is a really, really, really long time!*

When you had to sit on a wooden desk chair for fifty minutes at a time, seven hours a day, Monday through Friday, all year long, it could be total torture. Especially if the teacher was a real nerd and not the least bit entertaining.

It was even worse with a teacher like Mr. Mills, who spoke like he was talking in his sleep.

Only six more minutes till the bell rings, and football starts, Tiki told himself, sighing heavily.

Tick . . . tick . . . tick . . . tick . . .

Actually, it had been a really good day until this last period. All his other teachers were at least okay—and two of them, Ms. Simms, his Science teacher, and Mr. Kaye, his Math teacher, were a lot *better* than okay.

Tiki thought it was going to be a fantastic school year—until he stepped into Mr. Mills's bone-deadly World History class. Tiki was afraid he might die of boredom before the period finally, mercifully ended.

Tick . . . tick . . . tick . . . tick . . .

Only *five* minutes to go.

As Mr. Mills went on describing just how dark the Dark Ages really were, Tiki's mind wandered back to those dark looks between Coach Spangler and Mr. Pellugi. He wondered what they meant.

Maybe one of the Eagles' key players had suffered an injury—like last year, when Matt Clayton broke his leg at summer camp and missed the first part of the season.

Matt had come back just in time to help them win the championship, but Tiki could imagine how the coaches would feel if the injury curse struck again.

"In the year 1000, people took baths only once a year," Mr. Mills was saying. "That's why weddings traditionally happen in June—right after everyone's annual bath . . ."

Tiki felt glad that he lived in the modern age, not back in the Dark Ages. He could only imagine how bad people must have smelled back then.

" . . . it's also why the rich used so much perfume," Mr. Mills finished. "Any questions?"

Tiki's eyes went back to the clock on the wall. Why did they put clocks on classroom walls? he wondered.

It just made you think about being stuck in school on a beautiful day.

Tick . . . tick . . . tick . . .

RRRING!

Finally! Tiki grabbed his notebooks and his new textbook and stuffed them into his book bag. While the other kids milled around, talking to each other and blocking the aisles, Tiki tucked his book bag under his arm like a football and dodged his way between them, pretending they were defenders trying to keep him out of the end zone.

Classes were over for the day, and nothing—nothing— was going to keep him from making it to the locker room!

He sped down the hallway, drawing a whistle from an annoyed hall monitor. But Tiki didn't stop—he didn't even slow down. Not until he'd made it down the stairs to field level and through the double swinging doors into the boys' locker room.

"Hey, Barber's here!" someone shouted, and instantly, everyone got up and cheered, high-fiving Tiki.

"Welcome back, Ronde!" said wide receiver Fred Soule, clapping him on the back.

"It's me—Tiki."

"Gimme a break," Fred said. "How'm I supposed to tell you apart when you're not wearing your uniform?"

Everyone laughed, and Tiki couldn't help joining in.

He wished football season went on all year long.

Finding his way back to his locker from last year, he found that it was empty and waiting for him. On the bench in front of it was a pile of new stuff.

On top of the pile was a set of pads and a plain blue number two practice jersey. Underneath was a blue jersey with yellow stripes and numbers for away games. Beneath that was a white jersey with yellow stripes and numbers—that was for home games. There were two pairs of white pants, six pairs of blue socks, and last but not least, a new white helmet, with a blue number two on one side and that fierce blue eagle on the other side, its claws extended outward.

"Awesome!" Tiki said under his breath as he started changing. Somehow, he only ever felt well dressed when he was in his full football uniform. No other feeling came close.

He trotted out onto the field for the first time this new season, his cleats piercing the perfect green grass, a big smile plastered across his face.

"Hey, Barber!" a voice yelled. "Heads up!"

Tiki turned, and the sizzling spiral Cody had thrown him without warning hit him square in the chest.

Tiki flinched but somehow caught the ball cleanly and flipped it back to Cody.

"Nice catch," Cody said, nodding with approval. "Soft hands—I like it, I like it!"

With any luck, that pass would be repeated dozens of times this season, with devastating effect on their opponents. But Tiki couldn't help wondering what Cody would have said if he'd dropped the ball.

It didn't take long to find out. When Fred Soule, the Eagles' number one wide receiver, jogged out onto the field from the locker room, Cody pulled the same stunt on him. Except that Fred juggled the ball and dropped it.

"Oh, no! Hands of stone!" Cody groaned. "Better dip your hands in some glue, Soule."

"How 'bout warning me next time?" Fred said, annoyed.

"Gotta be heads up, yo," Cody said coolly. "If you're not ready to catch the pass, someone else will be ready to take your spot. Right, Barber?"

Tiki walked away, pretending not to hear. If Cody was going to act like a brat, Tiki wanted no part of it.

He sure wished Matt Clayton was still at Hidden Valley. It would have been so much more fun to be in the backfield with someone he really liked.

Ronde trotted out onto the field, wearing his new number five practice jersey. "Come on, Tiki," he said, "let's go watch the seventh graders try out."

Tiki was just as curious as Ronde to see what kind of new talent had shown up for tryouts.

And there was a lot of it. This year's crop of seventh graders was even bigger and stronger than the kids in Tiki and Ronde's class. None of them were as fast as the Barber brothers, but then, not many kids were.

The coaches saw Tiki and Ronde coming and signaled for them to hurry up. "I want you two to help work with these new guys at the drill stations," Coach Pellugi told them. "Don't take it easy on them, either. We need to get a real good look at them."

Tiki and Ronde led a group of seventh graders over to the rope grid, designed for broken-field running, Tiki's and Ronde's specialty.

Tricky footwork was important not only for a running back like Tiki, but also for kickoff and punt returners. And this year, Ronde was the team's number one return specialist as well as its starting cornerback.

Tiki noticed that Coach Spangler was hanging back with his clipboard, taking notes on all the new kids. He did that last year, too, Tiki thought, remembering how curious he'd been to know what the coach was writing about him.

Those tryouts had been the most nerve-wracking days of his life. It seemed funny to him now. How could he possibly have thought that, with all his and Ronde's talent, they might not make it? But while they were going through those anxious moments, it had been total torture.

These poor seventh graders were facing those awful moments now, he knew. Thank goodness he only had to watch, help them out, and give them encouragement.

"Don't worry about it, kid," he told one boy who tripped while hopping his way through the rope grid.

"Just pick yourself up and keep moving forward. Hang on to your spirit, now."

The boy nodded, not smiling, and kept going, finishing the course without any further slips. Tiki knew that his kind words must have helped. He remembered how important Matt Clayton's support had been for him and Ronde the year before.

Some of these kids would soon be his teammates. The rest, their hearts broken, would have to make other plans. Tiki thought of his old friend Jason, who hadn't made the team last year but had gone on to star in track.

You just can't let things get you down too much, Tiki thought. Funny, he sounded just like his mom. She was always saying stuff like that to him and Ronde.

"Play proud," she would tell them both before every single game—and she never, ever missed one. *She's our biggest fan,* Tiki thought. *Not everybody gets so lucky in the mom department.*

He saw Ronde giving some advice to another boy, who was small like the two of them and seemed close to tears. "Hang in there, dude," Ronde was saying. "Don't give up. Hey, I was smaller than you last year, and I'm on the starting team now."

The boy nodded and trotted off to the next drill station. Ronde came over to Tiki. "It's looking good," he said approvingly.

Tiki had to agree. The future of the Eagles seemed

bright. He saw future stars on offensive and defensive lines, at linebacker, and at quarterback, where a tall, thin boy with a super-strong throwing arm was drawing oohs and ahs from kids and coaches alike.

After about an hour and a half, Coach Spangler gathered the new recruits, gave them a speech, and sent them home. Then he led the returning team members into the locker room.

Everyone was sweaty and tired and aching all over from using muscles they hadn't used since last fall. But nobody started changing or went to the showers. Everybody's eyes were glued to Coach Spangler as he addressed the team at the start of their new season.

"Welcome back, boys," he began, looking them over. "It's good to see all of you, a year older, and hopefully a year wiser."

That got a laugh, but Tiki noticed that Coach Spangler didn't even smile. That wasn't like him. He was a tough coach, but not beyond cracking a joke or two with his players.

"I think you could all see today what kind of future this team is going to have," he said. This got a big, whooping round of applause. "I agree," he went on. "Those seventh graders are going to make a big contribution one day— maybe even this year.

"Now . . ." He paused, looked down, and cleared his throat. "You boys are going to have a great season ahead

21

of you, if you work hard. I think this team will be even better than last year's model—and there's no reason we can't win another District Championship; maybe even make a run at the State title . . ."

Another round of whoops and hollering. Coach Spangler waited, again looking down at the floor, as if he were weighted down by something heavy and dark.

"Now, you're going to have to work even harder than last year to do it—because unfortunately, I won't be able to be here with you."

A gasp went up from the group of stunned players. Tiki felt like he'd been suddenly punched in the gut.

"Coach Hendrik over at Cave Spring High is taking a year's leave of absence—he's having back surgery—and the district has asked me to take over for him this season . . . I think you know how much I hate to leave this team . . ."

He stopped, swallowed hard, and looked down at the ground again. The room was so silent, Tiki could hear the ringing in his ears.

" . . . but I really don't have much of a choice. It's, um, an honor to be asked to coach at the high school level, and . . . on the other hand, it's been an privilege to coach you boys, and lead you to the District Championship . . ."

Another silence. Suddenly, someone said, "You're the man, Coach."

And then, boys started chanting: "Coach! Coach!

Coach! Coach!" The chant echoed deafeningly in the locker room, and some boys started pounding on lockers, making a drumbeat to go along with the chant.

Coach Spangler swallowed hard. He held up his hands for quiet, and the noise died down quickly. "I know how you boys must feel," he said. "Part of me feels the same way. But I also know you can overcome this, just like you overcame every obstacle last season."

Yeah, Tiki thought, *but that was a different team. Half of us were riding the bench last year, like Ronde and me . . .*

"Will you be back next year, Coach?" Paco asked. He, like Tiki and Ronde, would still be at Hidden Valley, so it was a very important question.

"I don't know, son," Coach Spangler said. "We'll see what happens. In the meantime, your job is to devote yourselves to winning *this* year. I expect you all to give the new coach, whoever it is, your full support—just as you would if it was me."

"Who's it going to be?" Adam Gunkler asked. He was the Eagles' kicker—an eighth grader like Tiki and Ronde and one of their old friends from Peewee League.

Coach Spangler had spotted Adam as a kicking talent, giving him a starting spot as a seventh grader when most other coaches wouldn't have even let him on the team. Adam had come through with an all-star season.

"Nobody knows yet who the new coach will be," said

23

Spangler. "It's not up to me, so I can't help you there—but whoever it is, I'm sure they'll be up to the job."

"Nobody's gonna be as good as you, Coach," said starting fullback John Berra, who had played two years under Coach Spangler.

"Well, thanks, Johnnie B.," said the coach, looking down at the floor again. "I'm gonna miss all of you boys—each and every one of you. But I'll have my eye on you all—so don't even *think* about slacking off. Now get back out there and give me ten laps for a final send-off!"

Everyone just sat there, stunned. A couple of kids started to protest, but Coach Spangler wasn't having any of it. "Let's go! Let's go!" he barked, clapping his hands. "Lemme see some hustle!"

Slowly, gradually, the team members got up and jogged off down the field. Some were shaking their heads in bewilderment. Others kept their heads down in silence. A few muttered to one another about how unfair it was.

But Tiki just sat there on the bench, stunned. He looked over and saw that Ronde was as frozen as a statue.

Tiki knew what his twin was thinking—the same thing *he* was: How were they going to have a winning team without the winningest coach in Hidden Valley history?

CHAPTER THREE
TROUBLED TIMES

"YOUR SHIRT IS ON BACKWARD, TIKI," RONDE SAID AS they shuffled out of the locker room after showering and changing.

"So what?" Tiki said in a dull voice. "And anyhow, yours is on inside out."

Ronde looked down and was surprised to see that it was true. He'd been so distracted and upset by the bad news that he hadn't even been paying attention.

"You should tie your shoelaces too," Tiki said. "You're gonna trip over them."

"Man," Ronde said, shaking his head as he bent down to tie them, "I sure wasn't expecting this."

"Me neither."

"You think they'll find somebody good?"

Tiki shrugged. "How do I know? Do I look like a fortune-teller?"

"Man, I feel sick."

"I'll tell you this much. Whoever they *do* get to be the coach, he won't be half as good."

"You got that right. Nobody could be as good as Coach Spangler."

Paco came lumbering up behind them. "Hey, dudes," he said, breathing hard. "Does this stink, or what?"

"I don't even want to talk about it," Ronde said.

"Me neither," Tiki added.

They rode all the way home on the late bus without saying a single word to each other. And when Mrs. Barber asked the twins how the first day of school had gone, neither one had the energy to answer her.

"I *know* you boys heard my question," she said. "And I *know* you're not being rude. No boy of mine is gonna be rude to his mother and get away with it."

"It stunk, Mom," Ronde muttered. "It was the worst day ever, okay?"

Her expression softened in an instant. "Why? What went wrong, Ronde?" She put an arm around each of the boys' shoulders and sat down between them on the stairs.

"Our football coach is leaving," Tiki explained. "Without him, we'll *never* win the championship."

"Now, how do you know that?" she challenged. "The season hasn't even started."

"He's right," Ronde said. "We're goners without Coach Spangler. He's the best."

"Was," Tiki corrected him.

"You know, your team is sure to lose if all the players

26

get as down as you two. How do you expect to win without any fighting spirit? Where's your pride?"

Ronde and Tiki were silent, looking down at their feet. They both knew she was right.

But it was easier to *say* "get your fighting spirit up," than to actually *do* it—especially when you felt like you'd just been run over by a ten-ton truck.

"Listen to this," Tiki said as he leafed through the morning edition of the *Roanoke Reporter*, the local newspaper. "'New Cave Spring Football Coach a Proven Winner.'"

The paper was delivered to their house every Wednesday morning. If there was already a story about Coach Spangler in it, the decision must have been made before the school year even started.

Ronde remembered the look on Coach Spangler's face the morning before. He must have already spoken to the paper's reporter by then.

"'Steve Spangler, longtime football coach of the District Champion Eagles of Hidden Valley Junior High School, has been hired to replace Coach Damian Hendrik of the Cave Spring High School Hawks, effective immediately. Members of the Hawks were all extremely excited about the hiring.

"'"Coach Spangler's the greatest," said the Hawks' second-string quarterback Matt Clayton, last year's all-star quarterback for the Eagles. "I should know—I played

27

for him for three years. He taught me everything I know, and I couldn't be happier that he's coming here.""'"

Tiki looked up and frowned. "Man," he said, "that's nice for him. But what about *us*?"

"Yeah," Ronde agreed, "he could at least have said something when we were practicing the other day." He felt annoyed at Matt, even though he could understand his friend's excitement.

"Maybe he didn't know then," Tiki said, getting up from the table. "It's amazing how fast stuff gets around, though."

"Uh-huh," Ronde agreed. "Looks like we were the last ones to know."

"You got that right. Nobody thinks about the younger kids."

"They'll probably hire the school custodian to be our new coach," Ronde said bitterly.

Tiki made a disgusted face. "I wouldn't be the least bit surprised."

"Cover two! Cover two!"

Hearing Coach Pellugi's call, Ronde shifted his position in the backfield for the upcoming play. "Cover two" was the standard defense for a pass play.

Coach Pellugi, the Eagles' defensive coach, had been running practices over the last two days. The routine was identical to what they'd done preseason last year, but the mood was totally different.

"Hut! Hut-hut!" Cody shouted, and the center snapped the ball. The wide receivers took off downfield. Ronde's man, a seventh grader brand new to the team, faked to the outside, then went long.

Ronde figured he'd have no problem keeping up—after all, he and Tiki were the fastest ones on the team. But the new kid already had two steps on him and was gaining ground when Cody's pass fell into his arms in perfect stride.

Ronde was beaten, and he knew it. Still, he knew he could chase this kid down if he really gave it everything he had—but he just didn't have it in him. Not in his heart. Not today.

"Barber!" Coach Pellugi barked at him. "Sit yourself on the bench and take a rest until you decide you're ready to play!"

The blood rushed to Ronde's face as he trotted over to the sideline and sat down. He left his helmet on, not wanting anyone to see how upset he was. He *hated* being yelled at—especially in front of people.

Coach Pellugi was much harder on his players than Coach Spangler, thought Ronde. But somehow, that didn't make them want to play harder for him. It just made them feel bad about themselves.

Tiki came over and sat down next to him. "Forget it, Ronde," he said. "He's not even the real coach."

"Yes he is," Ronde replied. "At least till they name

somebody else. And Coach Spangler told us to listen to our coach, whoever it is."

"I guess you're right . . ." Tiki sighed. "I hope they find somebody soon. We've got a game to play next week! We'll never be ready, the way we're going."

It was true, Ronde thought. None of the veteran players was putting his heart into practices. It was like they were all waiting for the new coach to come and rescue them.

If Matt Clayton was still here, Ronde thought, he would have rallied the team behind him and got their spirits back up.

Ronde wished he could be a leader like that. But he wasn't the kind to stand up in front of people and make a speech. Ronde liked to let his game speak for him.

The trouble was, he was *off* his game at the moment. They *all* were.

After practice that day, talk among the Eagles turned to who might be picked as the new head coach.

"It's gonna be Mr. Pellugi," Paco said. "Why else would they let him run the show in the meantime?"

"If they were gonna pick him, why'd they bother to do a search?" Adam pointed out. "I know they interviewed a couple coaches from out of town."

"Right, that guy from Blacksburg—what was his name?" John Berra asked.

"And the assistant coach from North Side High," Fred Soule added.

"They interviewed my cousin Nels, too," Cody said. "I bet they pick him. He was a linebacker at Clemson, and he's coached winning teams at Ashville High for two years."

Ronde sure hoped they didn't pick Cody's cousin. Cody was stuck up enough as it was—with his cousin as the coach, he could, and would, get away with just about *anything*. And he would get all the playing time, too.

Ronde and Tiki looked one another in the eye. They didn't say a word, but then, they didn't have to. As always, each knew what the other was thinking—that the Eagles' season was hanging in the balance and that everything was riding on who the new coach would turn out to be.

CHAPTER FOUR

THE NEW GUY

ON FRIDAY MORNING, THERE WAS A "WELCOME BACK" assembly. The school's principal, Dr. Bernadette Anand, rose to address the students.

"Welcome back, everyone," she began. "We're going to have another great year at Hidden Valley!"

There was polite applause, and some of the ninth-grade girls jumped up and yelled, "YEAH! WOO-HOO!"

"To begin with, let me introduce you to our new football coach," she went on.

Tiki sat forward in his seat, holding his breath. He looked across the auditorium, over to where Ronde was sitting with his class. Ronde had his eyes closed, and his hands were clasped in prayer.

Tiki knew what Ronde was thinking—*Please, don't let it be Mr. Pellugi or Cody's cousin Nels!*

"We've only had a week to search for a coach, because this situation happened quite suddenly," said Dr. Anand. "But we've found a solution we think will allow us to move forward. We won't have to go outside the school's family to find a great coach, because we already have someone in our midst who knows a good deal about football."

Here it comes, Tiki thought. *She's going to pick Mr. Pellugi, or maybe Mr. Ontkos, the offensive coach.*

"He was once headed for the ranks of NFL professionals before a serious injury ended his football career," said the principal. "Here he is, your new Eagles head coach, our own . . . Mr. Sam Wheeler!"

"Huh?" Tiki couldn't believe it. *Mr. Wheeler?* His old Science teacher from last year? The guy who used to throw balled-up wads of paper at kids who didn't pay attention in class?

Sure, he was a great teacher—much better than Mr. Mills, say—but Mr. Wheeler hadn't been near a football field in years! How was he going to step in, take over the Eagles, and lead them to a championship?

"Quiet down, please!" Dr. Anand begged as the hall erupted in cheers and chattering among the students.

Everyone had an opinion, and everyone's opinion was different. But there was one thing they all had in common: They were in a state of total shock.

"This is so messed up!" Cody complained in the locker room as they all got suited up for practice. "This whole season is going to be a total waste!"

"Come on, Hansen," Paco said. "It's not that bad. Wheeler's a cool dude."

"Oh, yeah. *So* cool," Cody mocked. "The guy has never

coached a single day in his entire life—not even Peewee League!"

Tiki liked Mr. Wheeler. And he remembered seeing him throw a pass to Matt Clayton, just for fun, that was the longest throw he'd ever seen.

Tiki wanted to tell the other kids about it, but he was afraid Cody would make him look ridiculous. What if the rest of the kids laughed at him? No, it wasn't worth the risk.

Then Tiki remembered how his mom was always telling Ronde and him to stand up for themselves. "Never be afraid to speak out," she would say.

So Tiki took a deep breath and said, "I think Mr. Wheeler might . . . work out okay . . ."

"Huh?" Cody turned to him in shock. "What did you just say?"

"I mean . . ." Tiki could feel the cold sweat breaking out on his forehead. "I mean, he was once headed to the NFL as a quarterback, right? He must know *something* about the game . . . don't you think?"

"Barber," Cody said patiently, as if he were talking to a small child, "playing is one thing, and coaching is another. They're totally different, okay?"

"I guess," Tiki muttered, backing down. There was no sense in arguing with Cody, because he could out-argue anybody. Besides, just then, Mr. Wheeler came charging into the room.

"Hey, team!" he said, clapping his hands sharply twice. "Everybody ready to hit this season running?"

If Mr. Wheeler expected a loud cheer, he didn't get one. Instead, a long, stony silence greeted him. The players looked down at the floor or away or anywhere but at their new coach.

"Listen, boys," Mr. Wheeler said, "I know you miss Coach Spangler. He's a great coach, and I know there's no point in me trying to be him. So you guys are going to have to get used to the fact that I'm the coach now, and what I say goes.

"I realize it's a big blow to any team to lose their coach right before the season starts. But we've got to live in the here and now—meaning *I'm* here, and the season starts *now*!"

He barked the word "now" so loudly that half the kids on the team flinched in surprise.

Tiki smiled to himself. He knew Mr. Wheeler's little tricks, his sneaky ways of getting your attention and keeping you focused. Something told Tiki that in spite of all the odds, the Eagles' new coach might work out just fine.

Mr. Wheeler watched practice that day as Coach Pellugi and Coach Ontkos ran the players through their paces. Afterward, while the boys were changing back into street clothes, their new head coach addressed them for the first time.

"Look, guys," he said, "I've got a lot of preparation to do, so I'm going to let Coach Pellugi and Coach Ontkos run the team for the season opener on Thursday."

A murmur of shock and surprise filled the room. Tiki heard Cody mutter, "Coach Spangler would never sit around taking notes while his assistant coaches ran the game."

Tiki wished Mr. Wheeler had heard Cody. If he had, he surely would have thrown a rolled-up ball of paper at Cody's head, like he sometimes did when kids fell asleep in his class.

But the coach must not have heard, because he went right on talking. "In the meantime, I'll be watching you practice, taking notes, and . . . well, you'll see what else. Good work today, and keep your chins up, Eagles. We're going to show the whole league how a good team can overcome a setback like this. You'll see. We're going to be fine—no, *better* than fine. We're gonna surprise everyone, and show them how it's done."

"Yeah," Tiki heard Cody mutter, "by finishing dead last."

Again, Mr. Wheeler didn't notice. "Before you leave, here's a final thought to chew on. This team is loaded with physical talent. From what Coach Spangler tells me, we're even deeper than last year, when we won the District Championship.

"But if we start letting negative thoughts take over

our minds, we won't be able to live up to our physical talents—because football is a *mental* game, too."

"It's not the game that's mental," Cody whispered, loud enough for the nearest kids to hear. "It's the *coach.*"

Obviously, Coach Wheeler was too far away to hear him. Tiki knew that if he'd heard, Wheeler would have nailed Cody with a paper ball right between the eyes.

"If you guys can accept the way things are and move forward," Wheeler was saying, "you can be champions again—maybe even go farther than last year. It's all about your mental preparation. So let's see how tight you can screw your heads on for Thursday's game!"

He clapped his hands twice, signaling that they were free to go. Tiki grabbed his book bag and joined Ronde as they headed for the exit.

"What did you think of all that?" Ronde asked him.

"I don't know, man." Tiki shook his head. "Everything Mr. Wheeler said is true, but I don't know if he can get the team to believe in it."

"Listen to this," Ronde said, holding up the *Roanoke Reporter* as they sat at the breakfast table the following Wednesday.

"'new coach named for eagles. Mr. Sam Wheeler, Science teacher for the past three years at Hidden Valley Junior High, has been named the school's new football coach, following the departure of much-loved Steve

"Spanky" Spangler for Cave Spring High School.

"'Wheeler has never held a coaching job before but was once a highly prized NFL prospect. Knee surgeries derailed his professional football career, but Wheeler believes he's learned enough along the way to be successful with the Eagles. "The talent is there," he said in an interview, "it's all about their mental game." Wheeler says he believes in the power of the mind to affect the performance of the body.'"

Ronde rolled his eyes. "If we lose, they're going to take this guy apart, Tiki."

"*Him*? What about *us*?"

"Yeah, you got that right," Ronde agreed, folding up the paper. "With him talking so much about the 'mental game,' if we lose tomorrow, people won't just think we're bad—they'll think we're *dumb*!"

The Eagles' first game was at home, against the Badgers of William Byrd Junior High, and the stands were packed to the gills.

Checking out the cheerleaders, Ronde saw that they were mostly returnees from last year. That explained why they had their routines so totally down. It was awesome, he thought, the way they could throw each other ten or fifteen feet in the air like that.

Everyone on the team was full of energy, hopping up and down, as Mr. Pellugi gathered them around on the sideline before the opening kickoff.

"Okay, boys, we've won the toss, so let's start off with a bang. We're playing a team that went four and twelve last season. We beat them pretty easily, too, as those of you who were here remember.

"But I don't want you to get overconfident. On any given day, any given team can beat any other. So don't take anything for granted, okay? Now get out there, and give it everything you've got!"

Ronde strapped on his helmet and ran onto the field to receive the opening kickoff. Tiki waited and watched, knowing his turn would come soon enough.

The kick was high and short, and Tiki thought Ronde would surely signal for a fair catch. But no—Ronde seemed determined to, as the coach had said, "start off with a bang." He caught the ball, then took a quick step to his left, dodging the flying leap of the fastest of the Badgers.

But because the kick had been so high, there were at least four other Badgers coming for him, and Ronde had no chance to get a head of steam going. Before he knew what hit him, he was flat on his back, and the ball was loose!

Players from both teams piled up on top of each other, and it took the referees a long time to peel them off the pile. But when it was over, they signaled that the Badgers had recovered the fumble.

Ronde got up slowly and walked off the field, yanking

off his helmet in disgust. Tiki could tell his brother was close to tears.

"Man, what is wrong with me?" Ronde said as he sat down next to Tiki. "What a way to start the season!"

"Hey," Tiki said, giving him a little shove, "remember what Coach said!"

"Which coach?"

"You know—Coach Wheeler. He said not to let negative thoughts take over our minds."

"Man, I don't know how to stop them," Ronde said.

Tiki was silent. He didn't know how either.

Things quickly went from bad to worse, as the Badgers pushed in for a quick touchdown and point after. It was 7–0, and the stands were as silent as a graveyard.

"Don't worry, Ronde," Tiki told him. "Look, now you get another chance. You can do it, man—just . . ."

"Just what?"

"Just, if it's a high kick, and you see you've got no room to run, call for a fair catch."

"You think I don't know that?" Ronde said bitterly.

"I didn't mean it that way."

"Yeah, whatever." Ronde trotted out, leaving Tiki sitting there, stung by his brother's anger.

This time, Ronde managed to hold on to the ball, even though he got practically nowhere against the fierce special-teams rush of the Badgers.

Now it was Tiki's turn. The offense trotted onto the

field, and Cody gathered them into the huddle. "Okay, forget about Ronde and his butterfingers," Cody told them. "We've got a game to win."

Tiki felt like grabbing Cody and shaking him. Who did he think he was, anyway? The big cheese of all time? How dare he diss Ronde like that?

"Look, Cody, you'd better knock it off," he started to say.

"You gonna argue with me, Barber? Or are you gonna play football?" Cody replied.

Tiki wanted to answer back, but he knew that on one level, Cody was right—they were in the middle of the game, and the clock was ticking down. If they didn't run a play, they'd be penalized—and that was the last thing Tiki wanted.

"Ohio State, on two," Cody said, repeating the play Coach had sent him onto the field with. Ohio State was a running play, where the halfback was supposed to run through the hole created by the offensive tackle's block.

Tiki took a deep breath as he got down into his three-point stance. His first run of the new season—he *had* to make it a good one!

Cody yelled, "Twenty-four . . . sixty-three . . . hut-hut!" and took the snap from center. He dropped back, then slipped Tiki the ball.

Tiki took it, put his head down, and charged straight ahead into the hole created by Paco, who had knocked his man to the ground.

Looking up, Tiki could see daylight, and he bulled forward until he was hit by the weak-side linebacker.

He hit the ground hard, with one, two, three, then four defenders piling onto him, knocking the wind out of him. They kept clawing at the ball, trying to create a fumble. But Tiki held on, gripping the ball for dear life.

Finally, the refs pulled the defenders off him. Tiki got to his feet and trotted back to the huddle, huffing and puffing.

Coach Ontkos sent Fred Johnson in with the play he wanted Cody to run. "Oklahoma," said Fred.

It was another running play for Tiki—but he still hadn't caught his breath! He wished Coach Ontkos had called a different play—a play for *someone else*.

"Okay," Cody said. "Oklahoma, on three."

"Cody, man," Tiki said, "I need a breather."

"Not now, Barber. After this play."

"But—"

"Hey out there!" Coach Ontkos called from the sidelines. "Quit jabbering and run the play!"

Shaking his head, Tiki, still out of breath, gave up the argument and got down into his three-point stance.

"Sixty-four . . . thirty-two . . . hut, hut, hut!" Again the snap, and again the handoff to Tiki. This time, he stutter-stepped, giving John Berra, his fullback, the chance to hit the line first. Tiki followed him, somehow staying upright as he was hit first from the left, then the right.

Berra blasted between the tackles and fell to the ground. Tiki leapt over him and into the flat. The whole field was open in front of him. All he had to do was run like his life depended on it! Except Tiki was now completely out of breath. His feet felt like a pair of stone pillars. He'd gone only ten yards when the linebackers caught up to him and dropped him.

"First down!" the ref shouted, and the chains were moved.

"Nice play, Tiki!" Coach Ontkos yelled from the sideline, clapping his hands.

But Cody was standing there in the huddle with his hands on his hips. "How do you not score a touchdown on that play, Barber?" he said, frowning. "You're slower than a snail."

Tiki was too out of breath to even answer. He just shook his head, turned, and waved to Coach Ontkos to take him out. Then he dragged himself off to the sideline.

"Hey! Where you going, Barber?" Cody yelled after him.

Tiki ignored him, taking a seat on the bench to catch his breath and recover.

He watched as Cody dropped back and threw a long bomb—but it was too long, way over the head of Fred Soule. The Badgers' safety picked it off and ran it all the way back to the Eagles' forty yard line!

Cody kicked at the grass, throwing his hands in the air as he headed for the bench. "How do you miss that,

43

Soule?" he yelled as they sat down not far from Tiki.

"What?" Fred replied. "It was ten yards over my head, dude!"

"Next time, get down the field faster," Cody shot back. "Man, you and Barber are a couple of slugs! You've gotta be the two slowest people on the planet!"

While the boys were arguing, the Badgers were running their offense. Tiki watched as Ronde dropped back in coverage, playing man-to-man on the Badgers' number one wide receiver.

The quarterback launched a long bomb. Ronde kept up with his man, stride for stride, and leapt into the air just in time to flick the ball away with his fingertips.

"*That's* my man!" Tiki yelled. "Yeah, Ronde! Way to knock it down!"

It was the first good thing that had happened for the Eagles that day, and it saved a touchdown on that drive, because the next two plays went nowhere.

The rest of the quarter was a defensive struggle, with neither team able to push the ball into the other team's red zone.

Finally, in the middle of the second quarter, the Eagles broke through. Cody hit Tiki on a short pass in the flat at midfield. Tiki knew the linebacker would be on him from behind, so he cut to his left, making the defender miss his tackle.

Tiki regained his balance quickly, putting one hand on the ground to steady himself. Then he darted forward through a hole between two other Badgers. He was at the forty . . . the thirty . . . the twenty . . .

Tiki was breathing hard. It was a hot day, and in his padding and helmet, sweat was pouring off him like water from a fountain. But he couldn't stop now. He could hear the footsteps of his pursuers, almost close enough behind to reach out and grab him!

He was at the ten . . . the five . . .

Tiki leapt into the air. The guy behind him must have jumped at exactly the same time, because he came down on top of Tiki's legs—in the end zone.

Touchdown, Eagles! It was Tiki's first score of the new season, and man, did it ever feel good!

He ran back to hug his teammates, and they all jumped up and down, forgetting the bad start they'd had. With the extra point, the score was tied, and it was only a matter of time before they overwhelmed the much smaller, slower Badgers.

But they didn't count on the one Badger who wasn't at all slow. They didn't count on his tremendous runback of the kickoff that followed Tiki's touchdown.

"Who is that little freakazoid?" Cody asked Tiki after they'd watched the Badgers' speedy number one dance into the Eagles' end zone. "He's barely five feet tall!"

Tiki frowned. He himself wasn't much taller. Lagging behind all their friends in their "growth spurt" was a sensitive subject for both Ronde and him—and Cody was anything but sensitive. He just said whatever came into his head, not caring how anyone else felt about it.

The first half ended with the score 14–7, Badgers. In the locker room, Coach Pellugi tried to pick up the Eagles' spirits. "Come on, team," he said. "We're better than this. We've got to get back our swagger and dominate these guys!"

Tiki and Ronde looked at one another. For some reason, Coach Pellugi didn't have the knack of getting the team psyched for a comeback victory. Kids were sitting around, not really paying attention. Even when Pellugi asked for a team cheer, it came out sounding totally lame.

"Where's Wheeler, anyway?" Cody grumbled out loud.

"That's 'Coach Wheeler' to you," Coach Ontkos said, his hands on his hips.

"Sorry," said Cody, not looking up at him. "Coach Wheeler. But I mean, shouldn't he be here?"

Sam Scarfone, their hulking defensive end, nodded in agreement. "I know he's new and all, but—is he even at the game?"

"He's in the stands," said Coach Pellugi. "Taking notes, I believe."

Cody clucked his tongue and sighed, shaking his head.

"Hey!" Coach Ontkos said. "That's enough of that! You just do your job, and let the coaches do theirs. You hear me?"

"Yes, Coach," Cody mumbled, frowning.

"Now, get your head back in the game, Hansen," Ontkos ordered as Cody sat back down on the bench.

Once Ontkos was out of earshot, though, Cody shook his head. "Great. This is just *great*."

Tiki felt a shiver go through him. He was worried, big-time, and not just because they were losing at the half.

It wasn't that he thought Mr. Wheeler wouldn't be an okay coach. But with Cody in this kind of mood, Wheeler might have a mutiny on his hands before he ever took charge of the team.

As the second half started, the Eagles yelled encouragement to each other. None of the boys wanted to start the season with a loss to the lowly Badgers—that would be worse than horrible; it would be disgraceful!

Adam Gunkler kicked the ball straight to the back of the end zone—but that pesky little runback specialist for the Badgers went back to get it and came out with a real head of steam.

He made the Eagles' players miss once, twice, three times, until he had only one man to beat—Ronde, who finally dragged him down at the Eagles' fourteen yard line. Three plays later, the score was 21–7, and the Eagles were in a deep, deep hole.

"Okay, I guess it's up to me," Cody said as the offense got up off the bench for their first series of the second half. "Let's go get 'em."

On first down, Coach Ontkos called for a quarterback keeper. Cody faked the handoff to Tiki, then ran with the ball around the end.

Tiki tried to get in front and put a block on one of the defenders, but the enormous Badger lineman knocked him backward, right off his feet, then forced Cody out of bounds.

"Come on, Barber!" Cody yelled at him back in the huddle. "Put a body on someone, will you? What are you, a total weakling?"

After an incomplete pass on second down, Coach Ontkos sent in the third down play—a crossing pattern with Fred Soule as the primary target.

Cody took the snap, looked downfield, then tucked the ball under his arm and ran with it. But since they'd seen him try a run on first down, the Badgers were ready for this gimmick. Cody was dragged down in the backfield for a loss. Now the Eagles had to punt again.

"What were you thinking out there, Hansen?" Coach Ontkos barked as the offense returned to the bench and the kicking team took the field.

"Soule was covered!" Cody explained. "I had to make a quick decision."

"Are you kidding? I was wide open!" Fred protested.

"Yeah, right," Cody said.

"Hey!" Ontkos shouted. "You're on the same team—start acting like it!" He shook his head and walked away to watch the punt.

This time, Adam kept the kick away from the Badgers' little speedster. Once again, the teams settled in to a defensive back-and-forth. The third quarter ended with the Eagles down two touchdowns and the Badgers driving for the kill.

On the first play of the fourth quarter, the Badgers' quarterback threw up a quick out into the near corner of the end zone. But Ronde was way ahead of him. He stepped in front of the receiver, caught the ball, and raced right back up the sideline. The Eagles, including Cody and Tiki, all screamed with joy, jumping up and down and cheering Ronde on.

"Touchdown!" Tiki yelled along with everyone else as they all high-fived each other. "Man, Ronde's having one whale of a game!"

They were still down a touchdown, with most of the fourth quarter left, and the Badgers would have the ball next. Tiki crossed his fingers, hoping he got another chance to score that day.

Luckily, the Eagles' defense held, and the team got the ball back for one more desperate drive.

Coach Ontkos called for a special play—the Statue of Liberty. Cody was supposed to drop back to pass, cocking his arm back with the ball—at which point Fred Soule, who had come around the end, was supposed to grab the ball and run with it behind Tiki's block, totally faking out the defense.

But when the time came for Fred to grab the ball, Tiki was shocked to see Cody pull it away and run with it himself!

What is he doing? Tiki wondered. Maybe Cody had just messed up, but it sure looked like he'd yanked the ball back on purpose!

If Tiki and Fred were fooled by Cody's move, the Badgers were not. They not only threw Cody for a loss, they made him fumble!

Luckily, the ball bounced right up into Tiki's arms. He grabbed it on the run, and kept going at full clip, right through the defensive line and straight down the field!

Someone was after him, he could feel it. He took a quick glance behind him, and saw that little pest gaining on him.

How fast is this kid? Tiki wondered.

The defender leapt and grabbed onto Tiki's legs. But even Tiki was bigger than this kid, and much, much stronger. Tiki dragged the kid along with him right into the end zone!

"YESSS!" Tiki roared as he got up and spiked the ball. The Eagles were now within an extra point of tying the game.

But Paco's long snap from center was high, and the holder, Joey Gallagher, couldn't get the ball down in time for Adam to kick it! Instead, Gallagher ran with the ball and was stopped just short of the end zone.

"Man, you really choked, Paco!" Cody yelled. "This team is so lame! I wish I went to another school. You guys are a bunch of losers!"

Paco looked stung, and Tiki could totally relate. He felt like punching Cody out. He was quick with the criticisms, all right. But not a word about his own fumble on the Statue of Liberty play! If Tiki hadn't picked up that ball and scored a touchdown, the game would have been over right there, and Paco's mistake would never have happened!

Tiki wondered if Ontkos knew what had gone on. Cody's Statue of Liberty fake-out had happened so quickly, the coach might have missed it or thought it was just a mistake. Tiki thought about telling him Cody had done it on purpose—but he figured it wasn't his place to tell on a teammate, no matter how much of a brat Cody was.

There were still five minutes left to play, Tiki told himself. Time enough to snatch victory from the jaws of defeat. And so he stopped thinking about it and watched the defense work as he waited to get back out on the field.

But as hard as they tried, the Eagles never got the ball again.

When the gun sounded to end the game, the horrible truth hit Tiki full force—the Eagles, at least for this week, were just another losing team. And at 28–7, it wasn't even close.

Looking up in the stands, he saw Mr. Wheeler packing up what looked like a big pair of binoculars. Tiki wondered what it was. He wondered what Mr. Wheeler thought of his team's first, disastrous game.

Oh, well, he thought with a shiver. *We'll all find out soon enough.*

CHAPTER FIVE

THE NEW WAY

RONDE AND TIKI WERE SUITING UP IN THE LOCKER room, along with the rest of the team, when Coach Wheeler came in. He was wheeling a TV on a tall stand, with another machine under it.

"At ease, gentlemen," Wheeler said as the boys dodged the TV cart. "Before we go ahead with the same old practice routine, I'd like to try some new things with you. I like to think of it as a 'new way' of preparing for next week's game."

He plugged in the TV and the other machine. "Gather round, team—we're going to watch some videotape."

"Videotape?" Tiki repeated. "I've seen that on the NFL games. Replay, right? It's cool—do you have slow motion?"

"I do indeed. And I taped our game the other day," Coach Wheeler said, turning on the TV and video player. "Let's take a look and see how we did."

"We *lost*, that's how we did," Cody said, and most of the kids laughed, even though it wasn't really funny.

Ronde could see that Cody was really beginning to get on Coach Wheeler's nerves. But the coach didn't call Cody out. He kept his cool, at least for the moment.

"I'm aware of that," Wheeler said. "But let's look at *how* and *why* we lost—so we don't do it again. At least this way, we won't make the same mistakes we made the first time."

Wheeler had put together a tape of all the best—and worst—moments of the game. He would show a key play, then ask, "What went wrong there?" Or he'd say, "Now that's good football."

Then he would explain, running the play over once or twice more, until everyone understood what he was getting at.

In the beginning, the boys were really into it. Even Cody was quick to volunteer answers whenever Coach Wheeler asked what went wrong with one of his offensive players. "Barber let a flea tackle him," he would say. Or, "Paco whiffed on the snap." Or, "Soule had a brain cramp."

Most of the boys laughed when Cody made one of his comments. But Ronde didn't think any of it was funny. He knew they were only laughing because they were relieved it wasn't *them* Cody was making fun of.

Well, sooner or later, Ronde was sure, they'd have their turn. Cody was an equal-opportunity joker.

"Hey, QB," Coach Wheeler finally said, stopping the tape after one of Cody's comments. "Why don't you give it a rest?"

"Just telling it like it is," Cody said with a shrug.

"Not in here, you're not," Coach Wheeler said. "This is my team, and I'm in charge. Got it?"

"Okay, Coach," Cody said, backing down. "Whatever."

Wheeler shot him an angry glance, then said, "How 'bout you give us a breakdown of what *you* did wrong, instead of criticizing everyone else?"

"I said I was sorry, okay?"

"Look. We've got a lot of tape to go through, and we're wasting time here."

"But are we gonna get out there and practice today?" Cody asked.

"Yeah!" some of the others agreed, and pretty soon, it was a whole chorus, clamoring to go outside and play some football.

"You'll get out there on the field when, and if, we get done with *this*," Coach Wheeler insisted. "Now calm down, all of you. None of you played a perfect game yesterday. You can still learn a thing or two from watching tape of yourselves, believe me."

They watched for another hour. Ronde got to see how his man had beaten him downfield by dodging Ronde's bump at the line. "Hey—I could avoid that by making the hit quicker, and with more force," he said to himself, making a mental note.

Like all the other kids, he wanted to get out on the field and move around. But he could see why Mr. Wheeler wanted them to sit here and do some studying.

When they were finally done, Coach Wheeler looked at his watch and said, "There's not enough time to go out on the field today. We'll get out there tomorrow and work on everything then."

A major groan went up from the benches.

"FOR NOW," Wheeler said, loud enough to make them quiet down, "I would like us to all close our eyes and breathe deeply. . . ."

"*Now* what?" Cody muttered under his breath.

Coach Wheeler didn't hear him—or if he did, he ignored Cody. "Concentrate on your breath . . . ," he told the players. "You're feeling all the tension rise up through the top of your head and the bottoms of your feet . . . now I want you to visualize next week's game against Patrick Henry. See yourself making all the right moves . . . scoring that touchdown, catching that pass, making that tackle . . ."

"Watching that videotape . . . ," Cody whispered, making the boys nearest to him burst out laughing.

"Shhh . . . ," said Coach Wheeler. "Concentrate on victory . . . see it in your mind's eye . . . see us all held together as a team with a big, giant rubber band. . . ."

Ronde heard sniggering from a few of the boys. He opened one eye and saw that Tiki was looking right back at him.

Ronde opened his other eye and glanced up at the ceiling, as if to say, "This is so weird."

Tiki winced. Ronde knew his brother liked Mr. Wheeler as a teacher and wanted him to succeed as the Eagles' coach. Hey, they *all* wanted that.

But Wheeler's "new way" didn't seem like the road to success to Ronde—and clearly, not to most of the other boys, either.

If he was trying to rally them behind him so they'd play their best, the Eagles' new head coach was getting off to a really miserable start.

Kind of like the team.

Out in front of the school, Tiki and Ronde saw their mom standing in front of the car. Seeing them, she waved and tried to smile.

Ronde knew she was trying to pick up their spirits and make them feel better. But nothing could erase the sting of the terrible opening-game loss—nothing but a resounding victory in tomorrow's game.

"Somebody's got to talk to Cody, man," Tiki said as they walked to the car. Tiki nodded his head in the direction of the quarterback, who was standing in the parking lot waiting for his own ride to show.

"Yeah," Ronde agreed. "You're right. Go on, go talk to him."

"Me?"

Ronde blinked. "You're not saying you think *I* should do it?"

"Yeah, man," Tiki said. "I'll back you up."

"How 'bout *I* back *you* up?" Ronde countered.

"Aw, Ronde, I can't talk to that kid."

"So? Me neither. He's way too . . . ."

"I know," Tiki agreed. "So . . . you gonna talk to him?"

Ronde did a double-take. "Tiki, man—it was your idea!"

A car drove up, and Cody got into it. "Now, you see?" Tiki said, shaking his head. "It's too late! Why didn't you go talk to him when you had the chance?"

Ronde sighed. Sometimes it was impossible to talk to Tiki. And if *that* was impossible, *forget* about talking to a kid like Cody!

Two long days had gone by. After practice Wednesday, the boys returned home, and Mrs. Barber already had dinner cooking. Ronde and Tiki were both hungry, and they settled right down to eat—their favorite, Mom's world-famous mac and cheese.

They were still annoyed at each other. All week long neither one of them had said anything to Cody. So instead of talking, they took turns leafing through the *Roanoke Reporter*, looking for the article about last week's game.

Because the paper only came out on Wednesdays, and the Eagles played their games on Thursday, it was always a long wait till they got to read about it.

Last year, it hadn't been that interesting reading about the team, because as bench players, they were rarely mentioned. But this year they were starters. And so this week, they both knew their names would be all over the article.

"Listen to this," Tiki said. "'The first game of the new era for the Hidden Valley Eagles was a huge, mistake-filled disappointment. The Eagles, a preseason pick to repeat as District Champs, lost to a William Byrd Badgers squad they should have handled easily. Worse, the Eagles had every chance to win, and didn't take advantage.'"

"What does it say about you and me?" Ronde asked.

"Now, Ronde," their mom said, "let your brother read." She had been about to dish out another helping for both her sons. But now she just stood there, as curious as they were.

"'New Eagles Head Coach Sam Wheeler says the team's first game may not be a good example of how they will play in the future. He says he is putting in a new system that should bring out the best in his team.'

""'I'm a believer in the mental game," Wheeler said, adding that the Eagles need to be the best-prepared team on the field, mentally as well as physically.'"

"Mom, did Tiki tell you we didn't even get onto the field at practice today?" Ronde said.

"What?"

"Coach just played videotape of our game and made us imagine winning," he told her.

"He probably thinks you boys aren't focused enough," Mrs. Barber said.

"That's right, Mom," Tiki agreed. "Coach Wheeler's really smart. I'll bet if we all just do what he says, we'll start winning soon."

"There you go," said Mrs. Barber. "That's the spirit. You need to get with the program, Ronde."

Ronde wished he could believe in it, but he had his doubts. Most of the other kids thought Wheeler was weird.

Sure, Cody had gone way overboard about him, but Wheeler wasn't exactly perfect. Ronde couldn't see how the new coach was ever going to get the Eagles to play their best for him—tape or no tape, mental game or no mental game—especially if he couldn't stop a kid like Cody from stirring up trouble.

"'The team did show flashes of greatness,'" Tiki went on reading. "'The Barber brothers, Tiki and Ronde—' Hey, that's us!"

"What's it say? What's it say?" Ronde asked, suddenly excited.

"'Although his fumble of the opening kickoff cost his team seven points, Ronde Barber ran an interception back the length of the field for a key touchdown, as well as batting away a sure touchdown pass from Kyle Martin of the Badgers. And his identical twin, Tiki Barber, had two long touchdown runs of his own.'"

Tiki looked up and grinned, and Mrs. Barber rubbed his head lovingly, planting a kiss on it, and then one on Ronde's head, too. "My boys," she cooed. "I'm so proud of you both."

"Thanks, Mom," Tiki said, grinning.

"Keep reading," Ronde told him. "I want to hear the rest."

"'Quarterback Cody Hansen, however, had his challenges in the game. His play, as well as the whole team's, will have to improve if the Eagles are to live up to their promise this year.'"

"Man," Ronde said darkly, "Cody's not going to like hearing that."

"It's the truth," Tiki said. "Let's just hope he takes out his anger on the Patriots tomorrow."

"You boys just focus on doing your best," said Mrs. Barber, doling each of them out another scoop of mac and cheese. "What do I always tell you, before every single game?"

Tiki and Ronde looked up at her and grinned. "Play proud!" they said, and slapped each other five.

"It's all Wheeler's fault," Cody said, crumpling up the paper and tossing it into the garbage bins filled with lunch leftovers. "Maybe if he was there on the sidelines with us, instead of hiding in the stands, you guys would've played better and not made me look so bad."

"Hey, man," Fred Soule said. "You're the QB. The buck stops with you."

"Wrong," Cody argued. "The buck stops with the head coach. Ask anyone." He looked around, and most of the kids surrounding him at the lunch table nodded their heads in agreement.

Ronde wasn't about to say anything. Like Fred, he didn't think Cody had played all that great. But he knew if he said anything, Cody would make him look stupid, and all the other kids would probably pile on, just like they did on the football field. Except for Fred and a few others, they were just a bunch of followers and would do whatever the leader did.

He looked over at Tiki, and Ronde could tell that his twin was annoyed too. But for now, Cody was the unspoken leader of the team, and everyone seemed to be falling in line behind him—or at least keeping their mouths shut. Like Ronde, Tiki was too afraid to speak out.

Except that Cody must have noticed the expression

on Tiki's face. "What, Barber?" he challenged. "You got something to say?"

Ronde could read his twin's thoughts. Should he say something? Should he back down? Ronde thought Tiki would be too scared to come back at Cody.

But he was wrong. "I think you messed up as much as anybody," Tiki said simply.

Cody's face grew red. "Maybe if I had a back who could block for me . . . or hold on to the football when he's tackled . . . or get with the program!"

"Yeah, shut up, Tiki!" Sam Scarfone said, getting up and staring down Tiki with his six-foot-tall, two-hundred-pound frame. "Quit dividing the team! We've gotta be united, or we're going down."

"Yeah!" a bunch of the others agreed.

Tiki looked to Ronde for help, but Ronde kept silent. He didn't want the team members ganging up on him like they were on Tiki.

Tiki frowned, grabbed his books, and said, "Later." He walked away, and Ronde went after him.

"Tiki, wait up!" he called after him. Tiki didn't stop, and Ronde had to run down the hallway to catch up with him.

"Tiki, man, I—"

"Why didn't you back me up, yo?"

"I . . ."

"You were scared!"

"Was not!" Ronde defended himself.

"What, you agree with them?"

Ronde shrugged. "Not really . . ."

"Why didn't you say anything, then?"

"'Cause in a way, I think Cody's right about Wheeler—sort of."

"What?"

"I mean, the video was *okay*—just kind of boring after a while. But that 'close your eyes' stuff is totally wack."

"It is not!" Tiki insisted. "Listen, if Mr. Wheeler thinks it'll help us, we should try it. I mean, he's the coach, right?"

"I guess. . . ." Ronde wasn't sure how in-charge Mr. Wheeler really was. "I'm not sure he knows what he's doing, Tiki."

"Well, don't you think we should give him a chance?"

"Yeah . . . but Cody—"

"Never mind Cody!" Tiki insisted. "He's just a kid, like us. This whole team is following Cody, when we should be listening to Coach."

"Yeah, well, whatever."

"Man," Tiki said, shaking his head and looking at Ronde, "you should think about it."

"I *am* thinking about it."

"You should think again, then." He sighed. "Well, I've got to go."

"Me too."

"See you after school."

"Yeah."

Ronde headed for his next class, shaking his head sadly. He and Tiki *always* agreed about stuff—well, *important* stuff, anyway.

But this time it was different, and Ronde felt miserable about it. Still, he knew Tiki must be feeling even worse. After all, Ronde had most of the team on his side.

In sticking up for Coach Wheeler, Tiki was pretty much alone.

Ronde stood at the goal line, waiting for the kickoff from Patrick Henry Junior High. His whole body wanted to tense up, but he told himself to stay calm, stay relaxed. The blood was pounding in his ears, and every breath sounded like a freight train inside his head.

He saw the ball rise into the air off the kicker's foot. It went up, up right into the setting sun. Ronde winced and shielded his eyes. Where in the word was the ball? It couldn't be gone.

No, wait, there it was! It was sinking back down toward him, spinning end-over-end. "Don't fumble," he told himself. "Stay relaxed . . . stay loose . . . catch it soft. . . . cradle it. . . ."

He caught the ball out cleanly and took off like a shot straight down the field. From every direction now, he could see the purple jerseys of the Patrick Henry Junior High Patriots closing in on him. Hands tore at his jersey, but they were going the wrong way, and his momentum made them lose their grip. Ronde veered to his left, then to his right, and then downfield again.

Behind the thunder in his ears that was his breathing and his heart, he could barely hear the Patrick Henry fans in the stands, screaming, "NOOOO!"

He raced down the field—to the forty, the thirty, the twenty . . .

"Ooof!"

He was slammed down onto the turf. But this time—unlike in the first game—Ronde held on to the ball!

He got up slowly, dusted himself off, and jogged off to the sidelines. He exchanged a high five with Tiki as his brother took the field along with the rest of the offense.

Ronde took a seat on the bench. "Nice going, Barber!" Coach Pellugi said, slapping him on the back. Now that Coach Wheeler was actually with them on the sidelines, Coach Pellugi was back to being the defensive coach.

Ronde watched as Cody took the snap from center, faked a handoff to Tiki, then ran a naked bootleg around to the weak side.

The Patriots were taken completely off guard, and before they could recover, Cody had turned the Eagles' excellent field position into their first touchdown—on the very first offensive play of the game!

As he crossed the end zone, Cody dove in, did a somersault, and came up dancing, shaking his hips as he showed off the football. Finally he spiked it between his legs and did a cartwheel before coming off the field.

The other members of the Eagles offense seemed to enjoy the show. After Adam Gunkler converted the extra point, putting the Eagles up 7–0, the offense jogged off the field.

As Ronde went back on along with the kicking team, Tiki passed him. "I can't take that dude," he muttered to Ronde.

Tiki didn't have to say who "that dude" was. Ronde already knew who—and why.

Ronde ran downfield on Adam's kickoff and took a flying leap at the returner. He knocked him to the ground— and the next thing he knew, he was at the bottom of a pile of players from both teams.

When he was finally able to get to his feet, he realized he needed to sit down and catch his breath. He signaled for Coach Pellugi to take him out for a rest.

Sitting on the bench and drinking a sports drink, Ronde overheard Cody telling two of his offensive linemen, "I'm going to carry us on my back today, no sweat."

"Hey, Hansen!"

Uh-oh. It was Mr. Wheeler, and he didn't sound too pleased.

"What's up?" Cody asked him.

"First of all, nice touchdown."

Cody grinned. "Yeah. Thanks."

"But easy on the celebrations, huh?" Coach Wheeler said. "There's no reason for any of that nonsense."

"I just thought the team needed a little boost of enthusiasm," Cody explained.

Coach Wheeler stepped right up to Cody and said, "And if you don't cut it out—right now—I'm going to take you out of this game! Understand?"

"Huh? Cut *what* out?"

"You know what I'm talking about—the disrespect. Don't think I don't know what you're up to behind my back."

"But—"

"No buts, kid. Just can it, you hear me? Or else!"

Cody scowled. "Yes, Coach," he said.

"Good," Wheeler said, and walked away.

Cody stared after him. "Or else *what*?" he said under his breath. "What's he gonna do, bench me and put the new kid in there? If he does, he'd better hope Manny wins the game for him. 'Cause if we lose, Wheeler will be the one who's in trouble, not me."

Wheeler must have heard him—or at least seen him muttering—because he spun around and got right back in Cody's face.

"Listen to me, son," he said quietly, staring straight at the quarterback, "I don't care if I have to put a raw rookie in there. I will do it if you don't get ahold of yourself—

and win or lose, this team will be better off. Do you hear me? Keep it up and you will be benched—and not just for one game, either."

Ronde knew Wheeler was right. Coach Spangler probably would have benched Cody already.

But he also saw Cody's point. Coach Wheeler didn't have much choice when it came to quarterback—not if he wanted to win this game.

Joey Bacino, last year's third-stringer, had moved to California with his family over the summer. The team had only two quarterbacks on its roster—Cody, and the new kid, Manny Alvaro.

Manny had a good arm, all right, and he was a good athlete, too. But he was only a seventh grader. He'd never even played Peewee League football, which meant he'd never really quarterbacked a team before.

Cody looked down at the ground, breathing hard, thinking it over.

Coach Ontkos had wandered over to see what was going on and had caught the last part of the argument. "Why don't you go out there now and prove yourself, Hansen," he said, "before you start broadcasting how great you are? Win us a game or two before you start strutting around like a circus clown. Remember what Coach Spangler used to say: 'Players win games. Teams win championships.'"

Cody looked like he'd been humiliated. His face was red, and he was holding his jaw really tight.

Coach Wheeler glanced out onto the field, then patted Cody's shoulder. "All right, that's over now," he said. "Let's get your head back into the game. It's fourth down, kid. You're on."

Ronde had to get out on the field to return the Patriots' punt. Luckily, it was a short one, and he was able to run it back past midfield, giving the Eagles good field position for the second time in a row.

Ronde came back to the sidelines, and saw that Coach Wheeler and Coach Pellugi were having a serious discussion while Coach Ontkos called plays for the offense.

Ronde moved closer and overheard Wheeler saying, "I don't know, Pete. Maybe this was all a mistake. Maybe they should have just given you the job."

"Hey, Sam," Pellugi said, putting an arm on Wheeler's shoulder, "it is what it is, huh? Sure, I wanted the job. So did Ontkos. But *you*'re the head coach. *You're* the boss around here. If you want to bench Hansen, Steve and I will back you up a hundred percent."

Wheeler shook his head. "Hansen's right about one thing, Pete—if I bench him and the team goes into a losing streak, I'm the one who'll take the heat for it."

"Don't let that punk kid push you around, that's my advice," Pellugi said. "You're being much too easy on him. If you believe in your way of doing things, stick to it."

"Thanks, Pete," said Wheeler. "But I don't want to crush his spirit."

Pellugi shook his head. "I don't know, maybe you're right to give him another chance. It does look like this game's going our way," he said as Tiki broke through the line and headed down the field.

"I don't know," Wheeler said, shaking his head. "Maybe I *should* have benched him. It's still early in the season. And Cody's attitude is affecting the whole team. If we get just one or two bad breaks, things could go south in a hurry."

Suddenly, a cheer rose from the Patrick Henry fans. Ronde's blood ran cold as he saw the reason—the ball was loose, and the Patriots were pouncing all over it! The bad break Mr. Wheeler dreaded had just happened.

Tiki had fumbled the football away, and the Patriots had recovered.

CHAPTER SIX

ROCK BOTTOM

IT ALL HAPPENED IN A BLUR. ONE MOMENT, TIKI HAD been in full control, darting through the defensive line and breaking into the backfield for a big gain on second down.

And then, suddenly, the ball was in the air; the world was upside down. Tiki found himself flat on the ground, staring up at two big Patrick Henry gorillas who were lying on top of him.

The Patrick Henry crowd was roaring. A whistle was blowing.

The gorillas finally got off him, and now his own teammates were looking down at him, frowning as they helped him to his feet.

"What happened?" he asked Paco.

"You fumbled, dude," Paco said glumly.

"Did they—?"

Paco nodded. "Come on, let's get off the field before they flag us for delay of game."

Tiki collapsed onto the bench. No one paid any attention—they were all too busy groaning and throwing their hands in the air as the Patriots scored a quick touchdown.

"You okay, Tiki?" Coach Wheeler asked, coming over to him.

"I messed up, Coach. I'm sorry."

"Forget it, son. It's still early. Get yourself together and let's go score some points!"

The Eagle offense trotted back onto the field. It was still the first quarter, and the score was tied, 7–7. But now the momentum was with the Patrick Henry Patriots.

On first down, Coach Wheeler called a crossing pattern, but Cody threw the pass behind Fred Soule.

"You cut too sharp, Soule!" Cody said as Fred came back to the huddle. "Next time, do it like in practice!"

"Come on, dude," said Fred, "you threw it behind me!"

"I threw it where you were supposed to be," Cody insisted.

Fred shook his head and sighed. Tiki felt for him. There was no sense in arguing with Cody, and no time for it, anyway. They had a play to run!

On second down, one of the Patriots blew through the offensive line and sacked Cody.

"Come on, you guys!" he yelled at his teammates. "Give me some protection here!"

It was now third down, and everyone knew the blitz would be coming. Coach Wheeler sent John Berra in with the play—Texas Tech, a screen pass for Tiki.

Tiki nodded with satisfaction—it was the perfect play to beat the blitz. He lined up wide, like he was preparing to block the blitzing safety—but at the last minute, he let his man get by. Tiki ran toward the sideline, then turned and reached out to grab the soft lob pass from Cody, which had floated over the heads of the blitzing Patriots.

Too late, Tiki realized that Cody had led him too far. He stretched as far as his arms could reach, but the ball skidded off his outstretched fingertips!

"Can't anyone around here catch the ball?" Cody moaned, throwing his hands up.

Tiki looked at the ground in shame as they trotted off the field, giving way to the kicking team. He'd been the key guy on two plays so far, and he'd messed them both up!

The game seesawed back and forth till just before halftime. No one had scored for the past twenty minutes. Every time the Patriots got close, the Eagles' defense held them off. And every time the Eagles' offense got near the end zone, their own mistakes and penalties pushed them back.

First it was Fred, flagged for illegal motion. Then it was Paco, penalized for holding. And finally, Tiki again, missing a key block on a pass play that led to Cody's getting sacked and fumbling. The ball was picked up by one of the Patriots, who ran it all the way back for a touchdown, just as the gun sounded, ending the first half!

Cody headed straight for the locker room. Tiki followed him. Neither of them wanted to talk to anybody right now. The rest of the team followed, but too slowly to see what Tiki saw.

As soon as they entered the locker room, Cody took off his helmet and threw it down in disgust. "This team stinks!" he shouted, kicking over a pile of plastic cups. "Can't anybody here play this game?"

Tiki picked up the cups and stacked them again before the rest of the team made it inside. *No sense in making things worse,* he thought. *Not now, when the whole team is down in the dumps.*

"Keep your heads up, Eagles!" Coach Wheeler said, clapping his hands as he came into the room. "We're only down by a touchdown, okay? We can still win this game. But right now, we're being our own worst enemy. We've just got to get our heads turned around!"

Tiki sat on the locker bench and stared at the metal door. He felt like crying. As far as he was concerned, *he* was the reason his team was behind. Sure, other kids had messed up too. But not like he had.

If they lost this game, the Eagles would be zero and two—and it would be all his fault!

Tiki came out for the second half with an angry attitude, primed to snatch victory from the jaws of defeat. He was ready to ram right through the defenders and knock them flat on their backsides!

Coach Wheeler's game plan against the Patriots had been to stress the running game, with Tiki carrying the ball a lot.

But because the Eagles were behind in the game now, Wheeler had to shift strategies. Instead of running plays, he kept on calling for pass plays.

And on those pass plays, Cody never looked Tiki's way even once!

Tiki knew why—it was because of that argument they'd had in the lunchroom. Cody obviously hadn't forgiven him for it, because several times, Tiki was wide open and calling for the ball.

But no—Cody would throw it up there, trying to hit Fred or Joey Gallagher way down the field.

"Cody, man, *give me the ball*!" Tiki begged midway through the fourth quarter, with the Eagles still behind by seven points.

Cody shook his head. "We need to get the ball down the field in a hurry," he said.

"Come on, dude!" Tiki moaned. "I'm wide open in the flat. Trust me, I can score off these guys!"

Cody sighed and looked Tiki in the eye. "This just isn't your day, Barber. You've got butterfingers. I'm going with what's working."

"You think this is working?" Tiki asked him. "We've

only got seven points, and we got those on a running play!"

"Yeah—*with me running*," Cody said, and that was the end of the discussion.

Meanwhile, Ronde and the defense were keeping the Eagles in the game, holding the Patriots scoreless.

With only three minutes left to go, and the Eagles on their own forty-yard line, Tiki finally persuaded Cody to look for him on the next passing play. "Okay, but don't drop it this time, Barber."

Coach Wheeler sent Fred Soule in with the play. "Penn State, on three," he told the huddled Eagles.

Penn State?

Tiki tried to remember what Penn State was. The Eagles hadn't used the play since last season and had never run it in practice. Tiki thought he remembered that it called for a fake handoff, followed by a quick pass to him in the right flat.

Tiki pulled off the fake, then turned to his right to receive the pass—only to see it whistle behind him.

"Barber! You idiot! You were supposed to cut *left*!"

"No, I wasn't," Tiki muttered, distinctly remembering he was supposed to cut to the right.

But it didn't matter, because now it was fourth down. With time running out, and no time-outs left, this play was their last chance to win the game.

Joey Gallagher ran the play in. "Miami, on four."

Uh-oh, thought Tiki. Miami was a trick play, a flea-flicker. It called for Tiki to take the handoff, then lateral back to Cody, who would throw a long bomb past the confused defenders to Fred Soule.

Tiki took the handoff without a hitch and got the ball back to Cody. But with defenders blitzing him, Cody didn't catch the ball cleanly. By the time he got the pass off, he was about to get creamed by a two-hundred-pound lineman!

The ball fell ten yards short of its intended target, and the Patriots took over with only fifty seconds left. Their quarterback kneeled down twice, and the game was over.

Incredibly, the Eagles had lost again!

And this time, Tiki was the goat.

The bus ride back to Hidden Valley School was miserable. Tiki and Ronde sat next to one another, but neither had much to say.

Ronde had played well—one of the few Eagles who had. But Tiki knew his brother couldn't enjoy it when the whole team was so down.

The season was only two games old, but it was already a terrible mess. How were they even going to make the playoffs if this kept up? Beyond losing, Tiki felt even worse about his own play. He knew he and Ronde were the most talented players on the team. But he also knew he hadn't played up to his potential.

Looking over his shoulder toward the back of the bus, Tiki could see Cody Hansen talking to a bunch of kids who were leaning in close to hear what he had to say. Every few seconds, one would turn and look at Coach Wheeler, just checking to see if he could hear them.

Tiki didn't need to hear—he knew they were all dissing the coach, blaming the team's terrible start on him.

Well, Tiki didn't think this loss was Mr. Wheeler's fault. Sure, maybe he wasn't doing a perfect job—he was new at this, after all. Tiki could understand why Mr. Wheeler might feel a little unsure of himself, having never coached a football game in his life.

But still, Wheeler wasn't the one out there on the field messing up. Besides, he'd really only taken over after the first game. So even if you did pin this latest loss on him, you couldn't blame him for the first one.

Besides, it wasn't Wheeler's fault that Coach Spangler had gone off to coach at the high school. They *all* wished Spangler was still there. But Tiki also knew that when you can't change things, you have to accept them.

Still, there were two things that he *couldn't* accept, and they kept eating at him. The first was his own poor play. How could he make so many mistakes in just one measly little game?

The second, though, was even worse, because it was

harder to correct. And that was the fact that, whoever's fault it was, the Hidden Valley Eagles weren't playing as a *team.*

It was Monday afternoon. All weekend, Tiki and Ronde had been in Charlottesville with their mom, visiting cousins. They'd had no chance to throw the football around. That really upset Tiki, because he was so anxious to work on his game.

All day Monday, he sat in classes without paying the slightest attention. His thoughts kept drifting back to the horrible game he'd played last Thursday.

When the bell finally sounded, ending the school day, he walked slowly down to the locker room. He was in no hurry to face his teammates again. He knew they all were probably talking about him.

Just as he was about to pull open the door to the locker room, it swung open, and there was Matt Clayton staring at him, smiling.

"Matt!" Tiki said, surprised. "What are you doing here, man?"

"Hey, Tiki," Matt greeted him. "I had to drop something off for Coach."

"Coach Spangler?"

"No, Coach Wheeler. He hired me to do a little job for him."

"What kind of job?"

Matt grinned. "You'll find out soon enough. Meanwhile, I hear you guys are having a tough time."

Tiki shook his head. "It's bad, Matt. I messed up big-time last week."

"Well, hey, cut yourself a little slack. Wheeler's a good man—he'll turn this team around, you'll see."

"I don't know," Tiki said. He told Matt about Cody's attitude, and how most of the players agreed with him.

Matt frowned. "Hmmm. That *is* a problem. Unless your coach and your QB are on the same page, it's hard to win. A team's gotta play like a team, you know?"

Tiki knew, all right. He couldn't have put it better himself.

"I wish Spangler was still here," Tiki admitted. "We all do."

"Yeah, he's great," Matt admitted. "But it doesn't do *me* much good."

"What do you mean?" Tiki asked. "I read in the paper that you guys are two and zero."

"True, but I've just been watching from the bench."

"Huh?"

"I'm only a freshman, remember? Like you guys last year, I've got to wait my turn."

"But you're the best quarterback to come out of Roanoke in years!"

"Thanks," Matt said, giving Tiki a clap on the shoulder. "Glad you think so. But I've got to be patient—just like you guys have to be patient with Coach Wheeler."

"Man, the paper's going to slam him *and* me this week," Tiki said.

"Forget that rag! When you win, you're the king of the world, and when you lose, you're nothing. I stopped reading about myself years ago, and you should too."

"I guess you're right," Tiki said. But he couldn't really see not reading the local paper—how else would you find out what was going on in town—especially when it was about *you*?

"Anyway," Matt said, "I'll be seeing you around—what with my new job and all. . . ."

Tiki went into the locker room, curious to know what Matt's little secret was. He'd said Tiki would find out soon enough. . . .

"All right, everyone," Mr. Wheeler said. "Today, for those of you who are willing, I'd like to try something new."

A groan went up from many of the players.

"I've got some very interesting video here—"

"Can't we play the game, not watch it?" Cody blurted out.

Tiki could see Coach Wheeler's face getting red. But before he could say anything to Cody, other voices started piping up.

"No disrespect, Coach, but we want to get out on the field!" said Sam Scarfone.

"Yeah!" a few others echoed.

"Look, kids," said Wheeler. "Let me explain something to you. This is not video of our last game. You guys know what you did wrong—and in case you don't, we'll be going over that with you on the field before our next game, I assure you.

"This tape is of *Martinsville's* last game. I had a former student of mine record it for us. You might know him— Matt Clayton?"

The name Matt Clayton caused a stir in the locker room. Many of them had played with Matt last year, and every one of them liked and respected him. But that didn't seem to change their minds about watching more videotape.

Wheeler cast an uncertain glance around the room. Tiki could almost read his mind. As a teacher, back in the classroom, Mr. Wheeler would never have tried to persuade his kids to do an assignment. Any kid who didn't fall in line would have gotten a paper ball thrown at him.

But as a brand-new rookie coach, Wheeler seemed unwilling to lay down the law to his team. Tiki wished he would do it, even if some of the kids didn't like it. At least it would have shown the team who was boss—the coach, not the quarterback!

Tiki saw the look in Mr. Wheeler's eyes. He was trying to be sensitive to how his team was feeling.

"Okay, look," he said with a sigh, "*I* happen to think

this tape could help us against our next opponent—but I understand why some of you might want to get out there right away and work on what you did wrong.

"So at least for today, I'm going to make this video session optional. I'll run the tape for those of you who want to learn from it. The rest of you can go out on the field and work with Coach Ontkos and Coach Pellugi."

Cody was the first to stand up. "Great," he said. "I'm out of here. Anybody else wanna get out on the field?"

Sam Scarfone got up, then Joey Gallagher, and then, seeing it was okay, several boys got up at once. Pretty soon, all but a few of the Eagles had left the locker room.

At last, Ronde stood up to go. Tiki shot him a surprised and angry look.

"Everybody else is going," Ronde whispered. "I can't just be sitting around here watching video."

Coach Wheeler stood there shaking his head and looking at the floor. There were only three boys left in the locker room—Tiki, Fred Soule, and John Berra.

Funny—they were the three who worked the closest with Cody; the ones he yelled at most when things went wrong.

Tiki shook his head in dismay. He knew why Wheeler had given the players a choice. If he'd demanded they stay, and they *still* walked out on him, it would have been the final blow to his leadership.

"Well, I guess it's just the four of us," said the coach. "So—let's take a look at the Colts, and see where we can take advantage of their weaknesses and protect against their strengths."

As they watched the tape, Mr. Wheeler would pause it and point out strengths and weaknesses of the different Colt players.

"Number seventy-seven tries to bull you over most of the time," he told John Berra. "If you let him by you, then give him a block in the direction he's going, he'll fall over his own feet and take himself right out of the play."

John laughed and slapped Coach Wheeler five. Tiki could see that John felt good having a secret plan, something up his sleeve against a tough opponent—and the Colts were sure to be that.

"Tiki, do you see the way they overplay the run? Look how they crowd the middle. You see it?"

He ran the tape back again, and again, until Tiki could clearly see the holes develop in the defensive line.

"We're going to run some plays early to the outside, until the Colts make an adjustment. Then we'll go back to the off-tackle stuff."

Tiki nodded excitedly. He could see just how the game plan would work, throwing the Colts off balance from the start. He looked up at Wheeler and grinned. "Got it, Coach."

"Good." Wheeler went on with the session, skipping

the parts of the tape that didn't apply to the small group of players in the room.

"Tiki, watch this," said Wheeler, cueing up a particular play and running the tape. "See how quick they are off the snap? If you run straight into that line, you'll get creamed."

Tiki nodded. He could see it was true.

"But if you wait for the play to develop and *then* make your cutback, you can break some long gains."

When the session was over, Tiki trotted out onto the field to join the rest of his teammates, smiling a secret smile. Most of the time, he liked to run straight up the middle, behind Paco and the rest of the Eagles' big blockers. But now, having seen the tape, he couldn't wait to try out his new bag of tricks on the unsuspecting Colts.

"You should have stayed for the video session," Tiki told his brother as they rode the late bus home. "It was awesome."

"Tiki, I really don't think a new trick or two will help our season that much."

"You're wrong, bro. You can learn a lot by watching tape of the other team—it's much better than watching our own games."

"Less painful, you mean," Ronde said.

"For sure. But Mr. Wheeler's really smart—he showed us just how to beat the Colts."

"If he was that smart, he'd know how to take charge of this team, and not put up with any of Cody's baloney."

"Who are you to talk about it?" Tiki pointed out. "You put up with it yourself!"

"So? So do you!"

Ronde turned to look out the window, and that was the end of the discussion.

Tiki shook his head. It was hard sticking up for Coach Wheeler these days. Even his own brother was against him!

CHAPTER SEVEN

ALL ALONE

"I'LL BET THEY FIRE WHEELER IF WE LOSE THIS NEXT game," Cody said.

He, Ronde, and about a dozen other team members were sitting at one of the long tables in the school cafeteria, eating lunch together.

"Maybe you should blow the game on purpose, just to get him fired," Sam Scarfone joked.

"Nah," Cody said, as though he thought Sam was serious. "That would totally tank our season."

"You mean it's not tanked already?" Paco asked.

"Not if we go undefeated from here on in," Cody said.

"Yeah," Ronde said, "like that'll ever happen."

"Not with Wheeler in charge," said Cody. "They should fire him. He stinks."

Tiki had just come over to their table, carrying his tray, and he heard Cody's remark.

"He does not stink," Tiki said. "He could be a great coach, if you all gave him a chance."

"Aw, stuff it, Barber," Cody said. "Keep your bogus opinions to yourself."

"I know him better than you do," Tiki said. "I had Science class with him last year."

"Hey, Barber," Cody said, "do you know the difference between Science and football?"

"Cut it out, Cody," Paco said.

"No, I mean it," Cody insisted. "Wheeler may know how to teach a class, but he's totally lame as a coach!"

"Just because we're off to a slow start—"

"A *slow start*?" Cody repeated. "Zero and two is not slow, it's pathetic! And look who we lost to—the two worst teams in the conference!"

"*We* lost those games, not Coach Wheeler," Tiki said.

"The buck stops with him," Cody shot back, and everyone at the table nodded in agreement.

Everyone except Ronde. He couldn't bring himself to join the crowd against his brother. But he couldn't muster the courage to stick up for him either.

Instead, he just sat there, feeling foolish and small, while Tiki took his tray and walked off to another table.

Ronde followed him. "Tiki, wait!" he called, but Tiki kept on walking.

Finally, Ronde sat down next to his brother at an empty table in the corner.

"You're a traitor," Tiki told him.

"I am not! I just happen to agree with them—Coach Wheeler's a bust."

"You don't *know* what he's like," Tiki told him. "I was at the video session Monday—you weren't."

"So?"

"So, he's having another session this afternoon—just in case any of you all decide to come to your senses and show up."

"We won't," Ronde said. "Everyone thinks watching video is wack."

"Well it's *not*," Tiki insisted. "You come and see for yourself today."

"I . . . I can't."

"Why not?"

"Because . . ."

"Because you're chicken!" Tiki said.

"Am not!"

Ronde didn't want to admit the real reason. Inside, he thought it might be cool to see your next opponent in action. But if he *did* go, the other boys would lay into him, exactly the way they were laying into Tiki.

Well, okay, maybe he *was* chicken. . . .

"Tell me you're not worried what Cody and all of them will say," Tiki demanded. "I'm right, and you know it. Well, I've got an idea, Ronde—why don't we switch uniforms, and you go as me?"

"What?"

"Pretend you're me, and go watch the tape. I'll be you out on the field. Don't worry, man, nobody will figure it out. And you'll get to see that Coach Wheeler is for real."

"You know what?" said Ronde. "That idea is so crazy, it's cool. Let's do it!"

"Barber . . . *Ronde* Barber," Ronde muttered in his best James Bond voice as he slipped on Tiki's number two jersey. Tiki flashed a wide grin as he put on Ronde's number five.

It never ceased to amaze Ronde that even their best friends had trouble telling them apart. The difference was obvious to him and Tiki. Maybe everyone else just needed glasses!

Tiki, dressed as Ronde, went out to the practice field, while Ronde, dressed as Tiki, stayed behind for the video session with about ten other kids.

It was a bigger turnout than the first time, but still, not that many. Ronde felt sorry for Coach Wheeler. His new job seemed to be completely beyond him.

"Hey, Tiki," Wheeler greeted Ronde. "Good to see you. No luck with your brother, huh?"

"Uh, no," said Ronde, feeling the blood rush to his face. He wasn't used to lying.

"So, let's go to the videotape," Wheeler said.

The coach skillfully pointed out the weak points in the Colts' defensive scheme. It was interesting, but Ronde started to feel impatient. He wished Wheeler would show more tape of the Colts' receivers so he could see how to defeat their moves.

"See there, Tiki?" Wheeler was saying. "Number twenty-nine, the free safety, tends to stay close to the line of scrimmage. He trusts his speed to get back in the play if it's not a run. So I'm putting in a fake handoff play where you stay in blocking position, then take the dump pass. Hopefully, the fake will cause the safety to drop back before you get the ball."

"Um, Coach," Ronde asked, "could we see some of their receivers?"

Coach Wheeler looked around the room. "Sorry, Tiki. None of our defensive backs chose to be here today, so I'm not going to waste our precious time on it."

"But—"

"I know you want to help out your brother—but if he's interested, Ronde can show up here himself. I've got lots of good stuff to show him."

Ronde bit his lip to keep from confessing the truth. He sat there, feeling like he had ants in his pants, until the video session was over.

He had tried to remember everything for Tiki, so he could share it with him later. But he wished he could have seen the *important* stuff—the players *he* had to guard!

One thing was for sure, though. Tiki had been right. Mr. Wheeler sure had a lot of great stuff to teach them!

He felt like telling everyone about it, but how could he? If he told them he'd *snuck in*, pretending to be Tiki, they'd all call him a liar and never trust him again!

. . .

"You were right, man," Ronde told Tiki over dinner that night. "Those sessions are some good stuff."

"I told you."

"I *said* you were right. Now don't rub it in."

"Ha!"

"What's this all about, boys?" Mrs. Barber asked.

Tiki told her the whole story, and their mom laughed out loud when she heard how they'd pretended to be each other.

"My goodness! You boys sure can make some mischief." She shook her head admiringly. "You know, if you ever change your minds about football, you could be great actors."

"No way, Ma," Ronde said. "Not me."

"Me neither," Tiki said. "We like football way too much."

"We'll never change our minds about that," Ronde echoed.

"Such talented boys," Mrs. Barber said. "I can't imagine where you got it from."

"From you, Ma!" they both said at once.

"Me?"

"Sure!" Ronde said. "Look how great you are at everything—work, raising kids, and especially, making mac 'n' cheese!"

They all laughed, and Ronde felt much better—better

than he had since the fight between him and Tiki started.

Most of the time, Tiki was wrong and he was right, thought Ronde. But this time, it was the other way around. And he, Ronde, had been grown-up enough to admit it. That felt good.

It didn't hurt that he'd given Tiki all those good tips from the video session. Ronde had the funny feeling Tiki was going to have a big, big game on Thursday.

"'eagles' season on the brink,'" Tiki read as they opened the sports page of the *Roanoke Reporter* on Wednesday morning.

"What's it say?" Ronde asked.

"It says Martinsville is our most formidable opponent yet."

"True," Ronde agreed. "The Colts had a ten and four record last season, and they're undefeated this year. What does it say about *us*, though?"

"It says we've played up to our potential . . . that we lost to a pair of teams with losing records. . . ."

"Man, the truth hurts," Ronde said, wincing.

"Wait, there's more. 'Coach Wheeler insists his methods have not yet had time to take hold. He said, "Soon I believe we'll see the real Eagles out on the field." The team's fans sure hope so.'"

"You don't have to read the rest," Ronde said. He knew what was coming. But Tiki read it anyway.

"'Running back Tiki Barber and several others suffered key lapses in last week's crushing loss to the Patriots of Patrick Henry Junior High. So far this season the Eagles seem to be their own worst enemy.'"

Tiki swallowed hard, and Ronde felt sorry for him. But Tiki was brave—he kept on reading.

"'Barber was not alone in his misses. The team as a whole has simply not played like a winning team. Their talent looks good on paper, but Coach Wheeler has not yet managed to make that translate into Eagle victories. Pressure is mounting on the rookie coach to succeed along with his team.'"

"Wow," Ronde said, shaking his head. "That's terrible. They shouldn't say things like that."

"Why not?" Tiki said. "It's true, isn't it?"

"Well . . ."

"Don't worry, Ronde," Tiki said. "This week, I'm gonna show them. I'm gonna show everybody!"

"That's the spirit, son!" Mrs. Barber said, giving Tiki a kiss and a hug. "You, too, Ronde. You boys play proud tomorrow, you hear me? You play proud, and turn around this season of yours!"

"We hear you, Mom!" they both said together.

CHAPTER EIGHT

TURNAROUND

TIKI FELT DIFFERENT THIS TIME, RIGHT FROM THE opening kickoff. On the Eagles' first possession, he took the ball from Cody on third and short.

But instead of bulling straight ahead into the line as he'd been doing all season, he just stood there, watching and waiting as his blockers wrestled with the Colt rush.

There—an opening! Tiki darted through it before the surprised defenders could react. He sprinted past the middle linebacker, who leapt at him, reaching. . . .

Tiki made him miss with a quick stutter-step, then spun clockwise and headed back across the field toward the sideline. Only one more defender to beat—and Tiki turned the corner just as the pursuer's hand made a grab for his jersey.

Too late—Tiki tore loose and sprinted straight into the end zone for a touchdown, on the Eagles' first possession of the game!

His teammates encircled him, jumping up and down. "Hey, man, slap me five," Cody said as they jogged to the sidelines. "*That's* what I'm talkin' about! Way to run and deke!"

Tiki slapped Cody's hand, but his heart wasn't in it. That play had been designed only to gain a few yards and a first down. Tiki had turned it into a long gainer only with the help of Mr. Wheeler's videotape—the very thing Cody had been trashing all week!

With the score 7–0, the Eagles' defense held, and the Colts had to punt. Ronde ran the ball back to midfield, and the offense took over again.

The first two plays—both passes—were stopped by the Colts secondary. Now it was third down and ten. The play came in from the sidelines. "Texas Tech, on four," said Tyrone.

Tiki grinned. Knowing from the videotape that the Colts would be blitzing on the next play, Coach Wheeler had called a screen pass with Tiki's name on it.

Tiki lined up and faked a block on the weak side linebacker, who was blitzing along with the safety. Then Tiki ran for the sidelines, turned, and saw the pass floating toward him.

He grabbed it in midstride—and waited for his blockers to do their thing in front of him. When the hole developed, Tiki spurted through it into daylight!

Once again, it was a footrace to the end zone, and there was nobody on that field—except of course for Ronde—who could match Tiki stride for stride.

Two drives, and two touchdowns for Tiki and the Eagles!

Tiki felt like he was floating on air—and he practically was, as his teammates lifted him up off the ground in celebration and carried him back to the bench.

Martinsville came back with a quick field goal, but the game was already out of hand for them, and it only got worse as time went on.

Tiki kept pounding out run after run. By the end of the first half, he'd scored a third touchdown, and had run for over one hundred yards—an incredible performance, and with half the game still to go!

"You da man, Tiki!" Paco said, clapping him on the back in the locker room at halftime. "Game ball for you!"

"No, Paco," Tiki said. "Save it—the game's only half over."

Ronde sat down next to his brother, all smiles. "You played some football out there," he said.

"Thanks," Tiki said. "It was all that videotape, man."

Ronde nodded. "I know what you mean," he said. "But now's not the time to fight about it. Just take it out on the field, and make the other team pay. We'll deal with that stuff later."

Tiki knew Ronde was right. There'd be time to straighten out the team's problems after the game. First, they had to finish what they'd started.

Tiki did manage another touchdown in the second

half, but it was obvious that the Colts had made some halftime adjustments. Everywhere he went, there were two Colts dogging him, and jumping him the second he touched the ball.

But that meant that on every play, somebody else was *free*. The Eagles scored another twenty points without Tiki touching the ball.

Tiki managed to tough it out, even though every inch of his body ached. By the end of the game, the final score was Eagles 44, Colts 13. He'd racked up one hundred forty yards rushing, seventy-five yards passing, four receptions, three touchdowns.

He couldn't wait to see what the newspaper said about him next week!

"We did it!" Cody exulted as they trotted back into the visitors' locker room after the game. He hugged Tiki. "Man, you and me, we're gonna turn this season around!"

So now Cody was making it out to be the *two* of them? *Well*, thought Tiki, *thanks for including me.*

"Hey!" he said, pushing Cody away. "You'd better give some credit to the rest of the guys—this is a team game, Cody."

"Yeah, of course, sure," Cody said, dismissing Tiki's comment. "I know that. But every team needs a star—and our team's got two of them!"

Tiki wasn't biting. "I think Coach Wheeler had a lot to do with it too," he said, standing his ground.

Cody snorted. "Yeah, right. That dingbat?"

"He's *not* a dingbat," Tiki said. "He's really smart—if you give him a chance, he could show you a thing or two."

The whole team had gathered around to watch the standoff. Their two best players, having an argument, right when they should have been celebrating the team's first victory of the season!

"It's Coach Wheeler who deserves most of the credit," Tiki insisted, loud enough for everyone to hear. "His video showed me how to beat that team."

Coach Wheeler was busy in the training room with Sam Scarfone, who'd twisted his ankle. But everyone else was there, and everyone's eyes were on Tiki and Cody.

"That's baloney," Cody said. "Take some credit, Barber. You and me, we're the ones who've got this team going!"

"Tiki's right, yo," Ronde said, getting up and standing next to his brother. "That videotape stuff is way cool. You can get a lot of good tips from watching the team you're going to play."

"Sit down, Ronde," Cody said. "Who asked you, anyway?"

"He can say what he thinks," Tiki insisted. "It's a free country."

"What does he know?" Cody said. "He never even went to a video session!"

Tiki looked at his brother. "Tell him, Ronde."

Ronde started to speak, then stopped and looked down at the ground.

"*Tell* him."

"I . . . I *did* go to the videotape session."

"No you didn't," said Fred Soule. "I've been at every video session, and you never went to one."

"Yes I did," said Ronde. "I went . . . in Tiki's uniform."

A gasp went up from all the players. Then some of them started to laugh.

"Hey, that's awesome!" Paco said.

"Masters of disguise!" said Joey Gallagher.

"I'm telling you," Ronde said, "you all should check it out. You'll play better if you do."

"Sounds good to me," said Adam. "Count me in."

"Me too," said Matthew Schulz, the middle linebacker.

Soon, all but a few of the players were on board. When Coach Wheeler walked in, having tended to Sam Scarfone's ankle, he was shocked to see his players were still in uniform.

"What's going on, men?"

"We've been having a little team meeting," Tiki explained. "Right, guys?"

"Right!"

Cody made a face, went to his locker, and started changing, ignoring the rest of them.

That's when Tiki knew the battle wasn't over, that he and Coach Wheeler still had their work cut out for them. Sure, most of the team was now on board. But if the quarterback and the coach couldn't figure out a way to work together—and fast—in the long run, the Eagles were doomed to fail.

CHAPTER NINE

REVERSAL OF FORTUNE

RONDE FELT LIKE A HUGE WEIGHT HAD COME OFF HIS shoulders. He was surprised that none of the other kids were mad at him for faking them out by pretending to be Tiki.

In fact, they all seemed impressed that the twins could pull it off. So impressed that they were willing to cut him and Tiki plenty of slack.

Still, it felt good to get the secret off his chest. Ronde wasn't accustomed to not telling the truth.

At the next video session, Mr. Wheeler showed them Matt Clayton's tape of their next opponent, the Rockets of North Side Junior High.

This time, the room was packed with players. Only Cody, Sam Scarfone, and a few others had stayed away.

"Okay," Mr. Wheeler began. "This is more like it. Yes sir, this is the kind of turnout we need to make us a real team, not just a bunch of players wearing the same uniform!"

He rubbed his hands together excitedly. "Now, North Side's strength is their defense, so let's begin with that. . . ."

The session went on for almost two hours. But when it was over, every player in the room had at least one thing to take away that would make him a better player in the upcoming game.

For Ronde, the key was to force his man to the outside as often as possible. Mr. Wheeler pointed out how the receiver had trouble catching balls and still landing inbounds.

"Too bad Cody wasn't here to see this," said Ronde afterward.

"Yeah," Tiki agreed. "He might have learned something."

"Gang, before we break this up, I'd like you to all gather around in a circle," said Coach Wheeler.

Ronde saw some of the boys casting doubtful looks at each other, but they all formed the circle anyway.

"Now join hands and close your eyes," Wheeler told them.

Ronde looked around to see who was shutting his eyes and who wasn't—it was only about fifty-fifty. Finally, he closed his own, figuring he might as well give Wheeler's methods a fair shake.

"I want you all to see us on the field, taking the game to North Side, dominating them from the first minute on . . . can you see it?"

A few boys muttered, "Uh-huh," or "Yes." But most

didn't say anything. Ronde nodded his head but kept his mouth shut.

"I'm going to make a prediction right now," Coach Wheeler said. "This will be the game that defines our season. If we can play as a team, I believe we will prevail. Are you all with me?"

"Yeah!" a lot of the boys said.

"I can't hear you!"

"YEAH!" they all shouted this time.

"That's better. Now answer me this—who's the best team on the field?"

"WE ARE!"

"Who's got game?"

"WE DO!"

"Who's gonna play smart?"

"WE ARE!"

"That's what I'm talking about!" Wheeler said. "That's what I want to hear! And that's what I expect to see tomorrow night, out on the field!"

Tiki and Ronde left the locker room floating on air. On their way to the late bus, Cody caught up to them.

"So? How'd it go?" he wanted to know. "Pretty lame, huh?"

"Man, you missed it," Tiki said. "It was awesome!"

"It was," Ronde agreed. "You should have been there."

"Hey, I'm a leader, not a follower," Cody shot back.

"That's why I'm the quarterback. I don't need any of that mental stuff to do my thing. I'm gonna let my arm do the talking tomorrow night."

They reached the bus, and Cody waved to his mom, who was waiting for him in a big black SUV. No rides on the late bus for Cody, thought Ronde.

"I'll see you guys tomorrow," Cody said. "Just one word of advice—especially you, Tiki. Don't let all that 'mental game' stuff mess up your mind, or you'll wind up choking in the clutch. Just get out there and follow my lead, and we'll mess up North Side big-time."

He walked away, and the brothers boarded the bus. "Man," said Ronde, "he sure thinks a lot of himself."

"I know," Tiki agreed. "I hope he still does after tomorrow. Because if he doesn't, it'll mean he played really bad, and if *he* plays really bad, *we lose.*"

The Eagles had North Side off balance from the start. Coach Wheeler had shown Ronde how to lateral the opening kickoff to Fred Soule. When he did, the onrushing Rockets found themselves overcommitted to tackling Ronde. Fred scampered free and set the Eagles up with a first down at the Rocket twenty-four.

But that was when Cody got to work. Not having seen the videotape, he didn't know that throwing passes up the middle meant that he was playing right into North Side's hands.

That was where their best players, the middle linebacker and the free safety, were positioned. The linebacker batted down Cody's first pass, and the free safety intercepted his second one in the end zone for a touchback.

Luckily, the Rockets' offense wasn't all that strong, and the Eagles' defense was well prepared for their two or three breakout-type players. They managed to stop the Rockets in their own territory and force a punt.

This time, Ronde faked the lateral, then tucked the ball in and spun around to the weak side. Sure enough, the Rockets, always overeager, went for the fake, leaving Ronde free.

He sprinted down the sideline, leaving the Rockets behind, and made it all the way into the end zone for the Eagles' first touchdown!

All over the field that first half, the Eagles were one step ahead of their opponents—except for Cody, Scarfone, and the few other holdouts who'd stayed away from Coach Wheeler's video sessions.

By the end of the half, Cody had already racked up three interceptions and was only four for fifteen in completions. The score was 21–14, Eagles, with two of their touchdowns scored by the defense.

The Rockets' two touchdowns had come on short drives, set up by interceptions.

In the locker room at halftime, Coach Wheeler came

over to Cody, who was toweling off next to Tiki and Ronde.

"Hansen," Wheeler said.

"What?"

"This half, for as long as we're ahead, we're going to feature the running game, and eat up the clock."

"Why, because of the interceptions?" Cody asked, annoyed. "Don't blame me for those—Fred and Joey can't hold on to the ball!"

Fred and Joey were both standing nearby. They looked at each other, then at Coach Wheeler, to see if he would stand for Cody's trashing them.

He didn't. "Hansen, I'm telling you right now, this kind of stuff has got to stop. The next time I hear it, you're heading for the bench, understand?"

Cody seemed like he was about to argue, but he must have thought better of it. "Whatever," he muttered.

"Not whatever," said Wheeler. "It's 'yes, Coach.'"

"Yes, Coach," Cody said, rolling his eyes.

"Now, look," the coach went on, addressing the whole team now. "We're playing a pretty good game overall. But don't think North Side is going to lay down and die, because they're not, I promise you. Everybody stay alert, and take care of your own assignments. No improvising!" He shot one more look at Cody. "Is that clear?"

"Yes, Coach!" everyone said. Cody moved his lips like he was saying it, but Ronde could see his heart wasn't in it. He wondered if Cody really would stick to the coach's game plan—and if he didn't, what the coach would do about it.

Right away, it was clear that Wheeler was right—North Side's coach had made some key changes at halftime. A lot of the tricks the Eagles had used to throw them off balance in the first half weren't working anymore.

On the Eagles' first drive, they notched two quick first downs on runs by Tiki, putting the Eagles close to midfield.

Coach Wheeler sent in the next play—another run, but this time for Joey Gallagher coming around end.

But to everyone's surprise, when it came time to hand the ball to Joey, Cody kept it himself! He headed downfield but was quickly blindsided by North Side's defensive end—and coughed up the ball for a fumble!

Cody got up slowly, brushing himself off. He turned on his own blockers in fury. "Hit somebody, for Pete's sake!" he shouted as they came off the field. "I'm getting killed here!"

His blockers stared after him, not saying anything. But as they got to the sidelines, Ronde could see them all shaking their heads. They were all much bigger than Cody, but none of them was brave enough to stand up to him.

Cody was mad, all right. Steaming mad. And he got

even madder when, on first down, North Side ran a trick play—a flea-flicker that resulted in a touchdown that tied the game at 21–all!

It was Sam Scarfone who had missed the key tackle on the play. Sam, like Cody, had skipped Coach Wheeler's video sessions. If he'd been there, Ronde thought, he would have seen North Side's flea-flicker and known how to stop it. Because he'd missed the sessions, he was caught flat-footed.

Ronde knew that Sam was best friends with Cody and had chosen loyalty to his friend over what was best for the team—going to the video sessions like all the rest of them.

Ronde jogged onto the field and took the kickoff, but he didn't get far. North Side must have gone to school on his moves during halftime, because they were ready for him when he spun around and changed direction— and they nailed him at the twenty-five yard line.

Ronde ran back to the sidelines and was headed for the bench when he passed Cody, who was getting up and strapping on his helmet.

Just then, Coach Wheeler approached Cody. "Hansen!" he barked. "Stay right here."

"Huh?"

"I'm putting Manny in for this series."

"No way!" Cody protested. "You're taking me out for a rookie?"

"I want you to sit here and think about things," Wheeler said.

"Think about what?" Cody shot back. "About how our whole season's about to go down the drain?"

Ronde's jaw dropped. He couldn't believe Cody had just talked back to the head coach like that!

"Think whatever you want," Wheeler said. "But when you ignore the plays I've sent in, that's the last straw."

"I'm sorry, okay?" Cody backed down. "I'll run the plays like you call them."

"Not till I put you back in there, you won't," Coach Wheeler said, holding firm. "In the meantime, sit here, root for your teammates, and think about why I took you out of the game."

With that, Wheeler turned to Manny. "Okay, Alvaro—get in there and play some football!"

Manny, who had played only a couple of downs so far this whole season, could not contain his excitement. Clapping his hands together and jumping up and down, he yelled, "Okay, okay, okay—let's go, Eagles!" He darted out onto the field, so fast that the rest of the offense had to run full speed to catch up to him.

Cody threw his helmet to the ground and stamped his feet, but he could only watch as Manny, the seventh-grade rookie, proceeded to hand the ball off to Tiki.

Tiki ran behind Paco, straight at the North Side left tackle—just as Coach Wheeler had shown him on the tape. The left tackle was the big weak spot on the Rockets' defensive line, and he was flat on his back after Paco's big hit.

Tiki sprinted by, running straight down the middle of the field and taking it all the way into the end zone!

Everyone cheered, jumping up and down. Everyone, that is, except for Cody, who sat there sulking, angry that he wasn't a part of it.

On the Eagles' next possession, Manny guided them down the field, with Coach Wheeler mixing runs and passes to keep North Side's defense off balance. They got all the way down into the red zone—but then Manny overthrew Fred Soule in the end zone on third down.

"That's okay, Manny," Coach Wheeler said to the rookie quarterback as he came back to the bench, clearly upset. "Don't worry about it. Everyone makes mistakes. Next time you'll get 'em!" He patted Manny on the shoulder.

The rookie nodded, feeling a little better, and took a seat.

"Man!" Cody muttered, stamping his feet as he paced at the far end of the bench near Ronde. "If I was in there, we'd have had that touchdown!"

Ronde didn't say what he wanted to say—that Cody already had three interceptions and a fumble today and had no right to moan and groan about Manny's mistakes. Besides, they were up ten points now, and Manny had done a pretty good job, all things considered.

Everybody knew Cody was talented. You could see he had a fantastic arm and was big and strong to boot. But his accuracy disappeared whenever he was upset— and he got upset *a lot*!

Adam's fourth down field goal made the score 31–21, Eagles. But North Side, always a good team in years past, still had a few aces left to play. They turned a botched handoff into a touchdown pass, thrown right over the Eagles' other cornerback, Matthew Schulz's little brother, Andrew.

Luckily, time ran out before North Side could get their hands on the ball again.

"Thank goodness!" Tiki breathed when the gun finally sounded. "At least our season is still alive."

"Yeah," Ronde agreed sullenly. "But for how long? If this team doesn't get its act together fast, we're gonna lose another game—and that'll be the end of our season."

Tiki knew it was true, even though none of them had ever said so out loud before. If the Eagles lost one more game, that would make three. No team with three losses had made it into the playoffs in the past ten years.

They were two and two now. A record of ten and two would do the trick. Anything less, and they might be watching the playoffs as spectators. And with their number one quarterback riding the bench for bad behavior, what chance did they really have to go through the rest of the season undefeated?

"This can't go on any longer," Tiki said. "We've got to do something about it."

"Who, us?"

"Uh-huh."

"Like what?"

"I don't know," said Tiki, "but we'd better think of something fast if we want to save our season."

CHAPTER TEN

COACHING THE COACH

"MOM, CAN'T WE PLEASE STOP AT KESSLER'S?" RONDE begged, tugging at her sleeve. "I'm hungry!"

"And I'm *tired* of shopping," Tiki moaned. "It's been two hours already. Come on, Mom, we need a break!"

Mrs. Barber laughed and said, "You boys are outgrowing all your clothes—you *need* to go shopping!"

It was true, Ronde knew. Both he and Tiki were *finally* starting to hit their growth spurt. They were still two of the smaller kids on the team, but not for much longer. . . .

"We've been lugging these shopping bags all over downtown," Ronde protested. "Our arms are tired!"

"Yeah!" Tiki agreed. "We need lunch! We're growing boys!"

"You've got no problem lifting weights with the football team, but shopping bags are too much for you, huh?" Mrs. Barber said, her hands on her hips. "Oh, all right. Tell you the truth, I'm getting kind of hungry too."

"YES!" both boys shouted, and they ran down the street to everyone's favorite lunch and ice cream place.

It was two o'clock on a Saturday afternoon, and

Kessler's was just about full. The Barbers had to weave their way, shopping bags and all, between the tables to the far corner, where they were seated and given menus.

"Mom, see over there?" Tiki said, pointing across the restaurant to the lunch counter. "There's Coach Wheeler!"

"Where?"

"Right over there—see?"

"Oh, yes—my, my, he really looks like an Eagle, doesn't he? Just perfect for the team!" She looked at her sons. "Well, aren't you boys going to go over there and say hello?"

Tiki and Ronde got up and approached Mr. Wheeler, who was sitting alone at the counter, eating a sandwich.

"Hey, Coach," they greeted him.

"Oh, hi, guys," he said. "How's everything going?"

"Well, uh . . ." Ronde shot Tiki a quick look and knew that Tiki was thinking the same thing. "We're kind of worried, actually."

"I see," said Wheeler, nodding. "I know what's bothering you. It's Cody Hansen, isn't it?"

Ronde nodded. "Coach, if we lose one more game, we might not make the playoffs. And we aren't even playing like a team!"

"You think I shouldn't have gone with the new kid— Manny?" Wheeler asked.

"No, that was the right move," Tiki said.

"Yeah, Cody deserved it. But . . ."

"But what?" Wheeler asked.

"But . . . I mean, Manny's good and all . . . I mean, he's gonna be good someday, but . . ."

"You think our only chance is to get Cody straight. Right?"

"That's it!" Tiki said, grateful that Coach Wheeler had spelled it out for him.

"You think Coach Spangler would put him back in next week?"

"I don't think so," Tiki said. "Not unless Cody stops being such a jerk."

Mr. Wheeler nodded. "Right. But I haven't got any idea how to turn him around." He sighed sadly. "I guess I'm a good teacher but a lousy coach, huh? Funny, I always thought I'd be good at it. I guess you never know till you try."

"Come on, Coach," Tiki said. "Just act like you do in the classroom when one of us acts up! Come down hard on Cody until he backs down."

"It's different," Wheeler said. "In class, my job is to teach kids, to make sure they understand the lesson. But in coaching, that's not enough. You also have to be able to lead. And that means you have to be able to make kids *follow* you."

"But Coach," Ronde said, "most of us *are* following you. At least, we are *now*."

117

"Yes, all except the most important guy on the team. Cody has set himself up as the leader, and there doesn't seem to be room for the both of us."

He shrugged. "I don't want to start a rookie at quarterback when we can't afford to lose even one more game. But what's the alternative? To let Cody keep trashing everything I try to accomplish? Let's face it, if I bench him next game, and Manny fizzles, I'll get blamed anyway. In fact, I wouldn't be surprised if I got fired if we lose another game anytime soon."

"Coach, could I make a suggestion?" Ronde asked.

"Sure, Tiki, go ahead."

"It's, um, Ronde," said Ronde.

"Really?" Wheeler shook his head and smiled. "Amazing. Just amazing . . . anyway, let's hear it, Ronde."

"I think you should have a talk with Cody—privately, when it won't embarrass him. I mean, I know he wants to win as much as any of us do. Maybe he'd listen if you took the time to explain things."

"I know that's what Coach Spangler would have done if he were still around," Tiki agreed.

Someone cleared his throat behind them, and the boys turned around.

"Coach Spangler!" Ronde gasped. "What are *you* doing here?"

"Hey, can't a guy get a sandwich?" he asked with

a laugh. "Actually, I'm on a break from practice, and I thought I'd drop in for a bite to eat."

"Well, have a seat, Steve," Mr. Wheeler said.

"Thanks, but I'm getting it to go," said Spangler. "Listen, Sam," he said, putting a hand on Wheeler's shoulder. "You see these two kids here?"

Wheeler nodded. "I know. They're gonna be big-time players someday."

Ronde beamed, swelling with pride. Tiki was all smiles too.

"I agree," Spangler said. "And when they're done with that, they might want to consider being coaches. I mean, they're learning fast. That was some terrific advice I heard them give you just now."

"You *heard* that?" Ronde moaned. "Oh, no!"

"Don't be embarrassed, Tiki—you were totally right!"

"Um, it's Ronde," Mr. Wheeler corrected him.

Coach Spangler shook his head and smiled. "You boys are going to have to start wearing your uniforms all the time so people can tell you apart."

Ronde grinned, and Mr. Wheeler winked at him and Tiki. "Even *that* doesn't do the trick anymore," he said. "They sometimes switch clothes."

They all laughed. "Seriously, though, Steve," Mr. Wheeler said. "How am I going to talk to that kid? He's a handful—you know him."

"I do," Spangler said, "and I know how I'd handle

him. But you've got to do it your own way, Sam."

He clapped Wheeler on the back. "You can do it—I know you can. Get your mental game together, Coach." He looked at Ronde, then at Tiki. "If these kids can do it, so can you."

Ronde was ten minutes late, and in a state of total panic—he'd never been this late for a practice before!

On the Eagles, if you were late, you had to pay a fine. Not in money, but in some dumb stunt the other players would make you do, like wearing your winter coat to school on a hot day, or wearing shorts in the winter.

If only Ms. Rosa hadn't made the kids stay until they'd copied the entire algebra assignment from the blackboard. It was a series of formulae that Ronde kept getting mixed up, and he had to erase his figures and rewrite them a bunch of times.

By the time he got to the locker room, the entire team was already out on the field! He smacked himself on the forehead, knowing he would surely have to pay the price.

He quickly got into his practice clothes and had just finished tying his cleats when he heard soft voices coming from the direction of Coach Wheeler's office.

The office was in the hallway that led from the lockers to the field. Ronde had to pass the door on his way out, and he couldn't help noticing that it was open a crack.

The conversation was just loud enough for him to hear most of what was being said—and to know that the other person in the room with Coach was Cody Hansen.

Ronde was torn. On the one hand, he knew he should get out onto the field with his buddies and practice for the big game.

On the other hand . . .

He knew it was wrong to spy on people, to listen in on their conversations. But this was such an *important* conversation—not only for Cody and Coach, but for the entire team, and that included Ronde!

If they hadn't wanted me to hear, he reasoned, *they would have shut the door all the way, right?*

He knew he shouldn't be standing there, tucked into the alcove so that no one would notice him. But he stayed where he was, riveted by what he heard on the other side of the door:

"This team needs you to lead them," Coach Wheeler was saying.

"That's what I've been *trying* to do," Cody responded.

"Yes, but don't you see, if you're leading one way, and I'm leading the other—"

"Well, then why don't *you* change what you're doing?" Cody interrupted.

"Now, see, that's what I mean," said Wheeler. "Try to remember that you're still in eighth grade, okay? Kids your age need adults to help show them the way."

"Yeah, well, I've *got* adults showing me the way," Cody said confidently. "My brother, my cousin, my—"

"None of them have anything to do with this team," said Wheeler. "You think they know more about coaching than I do—you've made that clear enough. But none of them can help this team win once you're on the field. And if they think they're helping you by telling you not to listen to your coach—"

"They never said that."

"Oh? Then why are you doing it?"

"Because . . . well, because you do things that are so *dumb*!"

Ronde thought Coach Wheeler would start shouting at Cody. But he didn't even raise his voice.

"Let me ask you something, Cody," said the coach. "Do you care if this team wins? Or is it all about *you*— your numbers, your heroics, your own personal football season?"

"No!" Cody insisted. "I care about the team first!"

"Oh, really?"

There was a brief silence. Ronde wondered if they'd heard his heart beating. It was so loud he was sure they could hear it in the silence.

"It doesn't seem to me like you care," said Wheeler. "And I think if you asked your teammates, they'd say the same thing."

"Yeah, right."

"Quite a few of them have come to me and said so," said the coach.

"Who?"

"I'm not going to give away names, Cody. But football is a team sport. No matter how good a player is, he can't win this game all by himself. Not at this level, and not at any level higher than this. Maybe you got away with it in Peewee League, but—"

"Got away with what?"

"With ignoring your coaches, taunting the other team when you score, and blaming everything that goes wrong on your teammates instead of taking responsibility for it yourself."

"But none of what went wrong was my fault!"

"First of all, that's a lot of garbage. You've made your share of mistakes on that field, just like every other member of this team. And I include myself on that list. But if the quarterback doesn't take responsibility for what goes wrong, but only for what goes right, this team is going nowhere fast."

"I don't have to listen to this—," Cody said, and Ronde could hear him getting out of his chair. Ronde looked behind him to see if he could get away before they found him hiding there.

But he needn't have worried. Cody wasn't going anywhere.

"You'll stay right here until I say this conversation is

finished," Coach Wheeler commanded. "Now I'm going to be totally honest with you. We've got a two and two record right now. If we lose again, we might not make the playoffs. I wouldn't even be surprised if we had a losing season overall.

"But if you will go with my program, like the rest of the team—if you'll come to practice, attend the video sessions, and play things one hundred percent my way—I will stick my neck out right now and guarantee that this team will beat Pulaski on Thursday."

"If they'd hired my cousin to run this team—" Cody began.

"But they *didn't*," said Coach Wheeler. "They hired *me*. I'm the only coach you have right now, and right now is all that matters. Because if we lose on Thursday, even if I do get fired, it won't matter who the new coach is, because it'll be too late!"Another long silence, and Ronde held his breath.

"Now I will agree that a lot of the blame falls on me," said Wheeler. "I should have taken this up with you right away, the first time you refused to follow my instructions. I should have benched you then and there, and kept you on the bench until you decided to fall in line."

"Ha!" Cody laughed. "We would have been zero and four by now if you had."

"Maybe. But I don't think we'd be any worse off than

we are now. Manny might have made more mistakes, but his teammates would have played better behind him—because he wouldn't have been yelling at them every time they did something wrong."

Another silence—an even longer one this time.

"Don't you think every kid on this team wants to win as badly as you do? Don't you think each and every one of them is trying his best, even when he messes up?"

"I . . . I guess," said Cody, his voice softer now. "I never really thought about it like that. . . ."

"Well, now's the time to start," said Wheeler. "Think of every one of them as being exactly like you—wanting the same thing, trying just as hard, caring just as much, and feeling just as bad when they make a mistake. Now, how do you think they feel when you rag on them about it?"

"I . . ."

"Notice that not one of them has ever called you out for throwing an interception, or a badly thrown pass. You know why they haven't? Because they put themselves in your shoes, and they realize how miserable you'd feel if they did yell at you. Besides, they know it would only hurt the team. Do you see what I'm getting at?"

"I . . . I think so. . . ."

"It's not just what you do on the field, in the game. It's how you treat the people you count on to help you win.

A winning team has to be like a happy family—any bad feelings, any anger or resentment, has to be aimed straight at our next opponent. Got it?"

"Uh-huh," said Cody softly. "I guess I have kind of yelled at people a couple of times."

Now it was Coach Wheeler's turn to be silent.

"See, my dad, he always yells when I mess up at home. Sometimes it feels like I can never do anything right. That's why I love this game—it's the only place I can . . . I can . . ."

Cody stopped talking, and Ronde thought he could hear a sniffle or two from behind the half-closed door.

"I understand," Coach Wheeler said. "Hey, lots of people have it tough at home. But in here, we've got to leave all that behind. We can't dump all our problems on the guys we trust to have our backs out there, right?"

"Right . . . I guess . . ."

"Okay, then," said the coach. "For my part, I apologize to you, for letting things get so out of hand for so long. And I hope we never need to have this conversation again."

"We won't, Coach," said Cody.

Ronde opened his eyes wide. It was the first time he'd ever heard Cody call Mr. Wheeler "Coach."

"Now, I'm not going to tell you how to handle this with the rest of the team," said Wheeler. "I'm just going to say one thing—it's up to you to rally your troops and take them into this next game with the feeling that we're all a family—a real team, not just a bunch of guys who put on the same uniform every week."

"Got it, Coach," said Cody, sniffling one more time. "You can count on me."

Ronde heard chairs scraping, and this time, he didn't hang around to find out if the conversation was over. He tiptoed away from the door, then ran down the hallway and out onto the playing field.

He felt guilty for listening in, and he couldn't wait to see what Cody did next.

But most of all, Ronde felt better about Coach Wheeler—not just because he was a smart guy, but because he was finally acting like the leader of the Eagles.

Now, if Cody would only do what Wheeler wanted him to, Ronde was sure things would get better. He didn't know about Wheeler's guarantee of victory on Thursday, but he sure felt better about playing Pulaski—one of the toughest squads in the entire league, and the only undefeated team left standing.

CHAPTER ELEVEN

A FAMILY OF EAGLES

TIKI WAS PLAYING CATCH WITH MANNY ALVARO when Cody came out onto the field.

"Yo, Tiki, what's up?" he called, waving.

"Hey, Cody." Tiki expected him to say something obnoxious.

But he didn't. He came right over to Tiki and said, "Look, dude . . . I know I've reamed you out pretty bad a couple of times. I just want you to know—I'm sorry. It won't happen again."

Tiki shook his head in disbelief. "What did you just say?"

"I said I'm sorry, man. You didn't deserve that. We're supposed to have each other's backs around here, not be messing with each other's heads."

"I hear you," Tiki said, nodding, still stunned that this was even happening.

"From now on, I'm just gonna concentrate on helping the team win. I mean, it's not about me, right?"

"Whoa." Tiki realized his mouth was hanging open,

and closed it. "Yeah. Yeah, man. I mean, that's what Coach Spangler always used to say, right?"

"So . . . we move on from here, okay? No more trash talk from me—not to you, or to anybody else on the Eagles."

"Or the other team, either," Tiki added. "That hotdogging in the end zone stuff has got to stop. It just makes the other team want to beat us more."

"I get your point," Cody said. "It's fun celebrating, but the main thing is, you and I, and the rest of the team, we've got a job to do—*together*."

"That's the right stuff, man," Tiki said, giving Cody the team handshake—fingers locked, elbows knocked.

"Well," said Cody, taking a deep breath. "That's one painful apology down, a dozen more to go." He walked off, looking for other kids he'd been mean to.

Tiki stared after him. Maybe—if Cody could stick to his new take on things—the Eagles could come back from the dead and be the monster team the whole league was afraid of when the season started.

"Hey, Tiki," Ronde said, coming over to him.

"Ronde, you're not going to believe what just happened."

Ronde smiled—a weird smile, like he knew somebody's secret or something. "I'll bet Cody just blew your mind, right?"

"Huh? How'd you know that?"

"I'm psychic," Ronde said.

"Are you going to tell me right now, or am I going to have to bother you all day long?" Tiki threatened.

"Okay, okay," Ronde said, and told Tiki what went down between Cody and the coach.

"You shouldn't have snuck up on them like that," Tiki said. "That's just plain nosy."

"I know. I just couldn't help myself."

Tiki could relate. He looked over at Cody, who was face-to-face now with Manny Alvaro. They were exchanging the team handshake. Cody then clapped Manny on the back and ran over to John Berra.

"Hey, you know what, Ronde?" Tiki said. "I'm getting to like the new Cody Hansen."

"You think he's for real?" Ronde wondered.

"Call me a fool," Tiki said, "but he's making a believer out of me."

"You may be right," Ronde agreed, nodding. "He might just be for real. And wouldn't that be nice?"

Tiki laughed. "Nice? It would be awesome!"

"Yeah, you could say that."

"Man, I just did!"

"'last gasp for eagles,'" Tiki read, repeating the headline for Ronde and their mom to hear.

"Well, it's *true*," Ronde said. "If we lose one more game, we can kiss the playoffs good-bye."

"It's gonna be tough, too," Tiki agreed. "Pulaski's undefeated, and they've got these two running backs . . . I forget their names."

"John Miles and Chris Tullo."

"Yeah, that's them—they've been tearing up the whole league all season. If a team keys on one, the other one runs them right into the ground."

"Never mind the other team," Mrs. Barber said. "If you two boys concentrate on playing your best, you can beat any team out there, I don't care how good they are."

"Aw, Mom," Tiki said, rolling his eyes. "You're our mom—you *have* to say that."

"Yeah, mom, it's not just about us," Ronde pointed out. "The whole *team* has to come to play."

"Well," said Mrs. Barber, "you can only control your own actions, boys. Just say to your own selves, 'Victory starts with me.' And then, go out and, like I always say . . ."

"Play proud!" they all shouted together.

"Let me show you boys," Coach Wheeler told the team, "why Pulaski is undefeated. I'll start by saying, it's not their defense. We can score on them, all right—but *stopping* them is going to be tough.

"The Wildcats run a Wing-T offense. It's your basic T formation, with one running back off to the side of the QB, and the other directly behind him.

"So far, no team the Wildcats have faced has figured out how to stop them, because their quarterback has too many options.

"There are the two running backs, Miles and Tullo—everybody knows about them. Plus, they run a lot of quarterback keepers to throw teams off balance. And, of course, when they do go to the air, there are three fine receivers to worry about—all highly skilled players. It's impossible to keep them all in check."

Everyone held their breath. Was Coach really saying they couldn't win against Pulaski?

Wheeler stopped the videotape. "But there is *one* player we *can* key on to stop the Wing-T machine right in its tracks."

Everyone exhaled, relieved that their coach thought there was a way to win.

"*There,*" he said, pointing to one player in Pulaski blue. "Their left tackle, number eighty-four—Burt Golub. He's a two-ton tank. The Wildcats key everything around him. If we can take him out of the play, I believe their whole offensive scheme will collapse."

An excited murmur rose from the darkened room.

"So we counter with one defensive end—Sam Scarfone—and one linebacker—Matt Schulz. Your job tomorrow, on every running down, is to shadow number eighty-four. Wherever he goes, you two go—and you take him out of the play."

"But Coach," Ronde said, "doesn't that leave us one man short in coverage?"

"Good point, Ronde," Coach Wheeler said with a smile. "You're right—you and the rest of the secondary will have to play man-to-man all game. But I think you can handle it." He gave them the eagle eye. "*Can* you?"

"Yeah!" Ronde and the other defensive backs all yelled together.

"That's what I thought," Wheeler said, cracking a smile.

"Coach?" Adam said in a small voice, raising his hand. "I was reading in the paper that—"

"Gunkler," Wheeler interrupted him, "give me that paper."

"But—"

"No, no, no, just hand it over."

Wheeler took the newspaper, balled it up, and took a jump shot across the video room. The paper landed right in the wastebasket.

"Yesss!" Wheeler shouted. "Two points!" Then he turned to Adam. "That's what I think of the paper.

"Never listen to what reporters say about you," he told the team. "Their job is to sell newspapers, not to help you win. That's *your* job!

"Believe in yourselves, *unshakably*. I want you all to take the hand of the players on either side of you. . . ."

A week ago, there would have been a chorus of groans.

But now, the Eagles just reached out and grabbed one another's hands.

"Now close your eyes," Wheeler told them. "I want you to travel in your minds to a place of unshakable belief in yourselves. This team *cannot lose*. I want you to repeat after me—WE REFUSE TO LOSE."

"WE REFUSE TO LOSE!"

"NO ONE CAN DEFEAT US."

"NO ONE CAN DEFEAT US!"

"IF WE PLAY LIKE CHAMPIONS, WE WILL *BE* CHAMPIONS."

". . . WE WILL *BE* CHAMPIONS!"

"Now let's get out there!" Wheeler yelled.

And even though it was only a practice, the screaming Eagles roared out onto the field, ready for anything.

CHAPTER TWELVE

MAKE OR BREAK

THE DRUMS OF THE HIDDEN VALLEY MARCHING BAND
thundered, keeping time with the pounding of Ronde's
heart. Tonight was the Eagles' big night—the night their
season would take off like a rocket, or crash and burn.

Cody Hansen was soft-tossing the ball back and forth
with Manny. Well, maybe "soft-tossing" wasn't the right
word. Even taking something off the ball, Cody's spirals
had plenty of zip on them.

"That's it, Hansen," Coach Wheeler said. "See how,
when you take a little off the throw, it makes it more
accurate and easier to catch?"

Cody threw another one, smack into Manny's numbers.
"Like that, Coach?"

"*Just* like that." Coach Wheeler patted him on the back
and kept walking, giving last-minute instructions to his
players along the sideline.

Ronde shook his head in amazement. A week ago,
Cody would have been moaning and groaning about how
the receivers should be able to catch his passes, no matter
how hard he threw them.

It was like a lightbulb had switched on in Cody's head. He suddenly seemed to understand that nobody was perfect—not even him—and that everyone on the team was trying his best.

Ronde strapped on his helmet for the start of the game. He and Tiki butted helmets. "Play proud," they told each other.

They turned toward the bleachers and waved to their mom, who was sitting next to Matt Clayton. They stood up and cheered for Ronde, Tiki, and the rest of the desperate Eagles.

Adam kicked off to the Pulaski Wildcats. Ronde and the rest of the Eagles' coverage unit sped downfield. They all knew about Patrick Walsh, Pulaski's big-play receiver and kickoff returner. Ronde's job was to key on Walsh, no matter where the ball looked like it was going.

Adam arced the ball to the other side of the field, away from Walsh, where the second return man grabbed it. Most of the Eagles swarmed him, but Ronde stayed focused on his man.

Sure enough, the player with the ball ran across the field and handed it off to Walsh. Seeing it coming, Ronde leapt at his man and knocked him flat!

Pulaski's famous Wing-T offense went into action at their own twenty-two—but the Eagles' defense was ready for them. They all keyed on Burt Golub, the big left offensive tackle. Just as Coach Wheeler had predicted, that strategy forced the rest of the Wildcats to adjust on the fly.

The result was chaos. On first down, the whole pile was shoved backward for a loss of five yards. On second down, John Miles nearly dropped the handoff.

Third down, and Ronde knew it had to be a passing play. He also knew the Wildcats needed ten yards, so he gave Patrick Walsh a lot of room coming off the line. Then he hit him, a legal bump, just short of five yards downfield.

Walsh staggered. He put a hand down to right himself, then darted toward the center of the field. If the QB was going to throw to his man, now would be the time, Ronde knew.

Not even looking for the quarterback, he watched Walsh's eyes grow wide as his hands reached out for the ball. . . .

Ronde leapt, stuck out his hand, and knocked the pass down—incomplete!

Now the Wildcats would have to punt. Ronde dropped back to his own twenty yard line to receive the kick.

It came at him, a tumbling, short, end-over-end kick. Ronde ran forward, keeping his eye on the ball, even though he knew that the Wildcats were all coming straight for him.

He grabbed the ball and tucked it in firmly. There was no time to look around for running room.

But even without looking, he could sense someone about to hit him from the left. Ronde took the hit and was able to stay on his feet by bracing himself with his free hand on the ground.

He pushed himself forward, getting hammered left and right. Somehow, he kept his footing as he zigged and zagged downfield.

Finally, someone hit him so hard that he flew through the air, landing with two hundred pounds of Wildcat on top of him—but with the ball still firmly in his grip.

He had given the Eagles the ball at the Pulaski forty yard line—excellent field position. Out of breath but feeling fantastic, Ronde got to the bench with a little help from his happy teammates.

"Way to go, Barber!" they shouted, clapping him on the back. "That's taking it to 'em!"

Ronde sat there catching his breath. With sweat pouring down his face, he watched as Cody Hansen took the Eagles' first snap of the day from center.

Cody handed the ball to Tiki, who blasted through a gigantic hole in the line that Paco had created by totally crushing his man.

Tiki burst into the backfield, faked out two linebackers, and was off to the races! By the time the Wildcats' safety dragged him down, the Eagles were at the six yard line and knocking at the door.

Cody led his team back to the line, took the snap,

and faked another handoff to Tiki. With the Wildcats totally fooled, he spun around and tossed a soft lob to the weak side, over the head of the cornerback and gently into the arms of Fred Soule. Touchdown, Eagles!

"What a pass!" Coach Wheeler shouted as Cody and the offense trotted back to the sidelines. "Nice touch on that ball, Hansen!"

"Nah, that score goes to Tiki and Ronde—talk about some running!" Cody answered.

Ronde couldn't believe it—for once in his life, was Cody Hansen really giving somebody else credit? Or was it only a beautiful dream?

Ronde was about to pinch himself, but he didn't get the chance. Tiki plopped down next to him, breathing hard, and gave him a playful punch in the arm. "How 'bout that drive, Ronde?" he said, grinning from ear to ear.

"I like it, I like it," Ronde said, nodding and smiling back as they exchanged the Eagle handshake.

"Okay, Ronde, it's your turn again. Let's keep it going!"

This time, Adam's punt went straight to Patrick Walsh. Ronde had been barreling right toward him, but now he stopped on a dime and backed off. From watching the videotape, Ronde knew how shifty the speedy runback specialist could be.

Cradling the ball, Walsh avoided one tackle, then another. Ronde waited till he made his move, committing to the outside. Ronde, in perfect position, cut him off, forcing him out of bounds right in front of the Eagles' bench.

"Great job, Barber!" Coach Pellugi roared. "Way to play smart!"

Ronde beamed, and slapped the coach five. But he had no time to bask in his glory—he had to get back out there on defense!

Ronde watched his man in the huddle and saw Walsh nodding attentively at the quarterback. He even thought he heard him clap his hands together and say, "Yesss!"

Ronde guessed that Walsh was the play's intended target. He was also willing to bet, judging by his man's reaction, that it was going to be a long bomb.

So Ronde decided not to give him a bump at the line, but instead drop back a full ten yards, giving himself a head start on the lightning-quick Walsh.

Ronde paid no attention to the fake handoff, and he did not react to Walsh's quick fake to the left.

When the Wildcats' receiver put on a burst of speed, Ronde was ready for him. He matched Walsh stride for stride and turned just as he saw his man's eyes go wide. The pass hit Ronde right in the numbers!

Cradling the ball, Ronde dug his back foot into the turf to keep from sliding. Walsh's momentum made him tumble forward, taking him out of the play.

Ronde was now free to run. And there was never a

doubt in his mind that, with Walsh on the ground, he himself was the fastest player left on the field.

It was like running back a kickoff, except better— easier, because the other team was taken by surprise, and their best coverage unit was on the bench.

Hands tore at Ronde's jersey as he dashed by. They grabbed at his ankles, too, but no one got a firm grip on him.

He kept the ball tucked tightly under his arm and focused like a laser on the end zone. He was at the twenty . . . the ten . . . *touchdown*!

Ronde dropped to the ground, gasping for breath, and let the ball roll away from him as his teammates lifted him up, smacking his helmet and shoulder pads in a frenzy of joy.

Adam's extra point made the score Eagles 14, Wildcats 0. It was still the first quarter, but already, the pattern of the game had been set. The Wildcats had never trailed by this many points all season, and they didn't seem to know how to react.

Their Wing-T offense kept going nowhere against the better-prepared Eagles. And on the other side of the ball, the Wildcat defense couldn't seem to stop Cody Hansen, who was having the greatest game of his young career.

Every pass he threw was right on target and easy to catch. He led his receivers perfectly, as if they were inside each other's heads. His handoffs and fakes were crisp and effective.

And whenever one of his receivers dropped a pass, Cody didn't blame them or insult them. He put his arm around them and patted them on the chest, telling them it was okay and that they'd catch the next one.

Ronde could feel it—something had clicked for the Eagles, both on offense and defense. They were finally playing as a team—not last year's team, but a new one, with new leaders.

And all of them were on the same page—Coach Wheeler's page. Their mental game was sharp now, and that just made their outstanding talent play up to its potential.

And then there was Tiki, who was having another monster game himself. On the Eagles' next possession, he swung to the outside and rumbled fifty-six yards, for a crushing touchdown that had the Pulaski players slumping in disappointment and disbelief.

"They're beaten already!" Paco told his teammates excitedly in the locker room at halftime. "Totally defeated. Eagles reign supreme!"

"Don't be too sure, Paco," Wheeler said. "Pulaski's still a good team, and their coach will make adjustments for the second half. You guys have to be ready. If they change their game plan, so will we."

He drew some Xs and Os to show them alternate formations, and then said, "We may even go with a zone defense if they drop the Wing-T."

But that didn't happen. Pulaski had gone four and zero with its Wing-T, and one scoreless half was not about to make them change their ways.

"That's a mistake," Ronde told himself. "Coach Wheeler would have changed everything up. He's really good at strategy."

And so the rout continued. Cody threw a long bomb to Fred early in the third quarter for another touchdown. Then, after Pulaski came back with a long field goal, Cody found Tiki on a screen pass that turned into a long gainer, followed by a chip shot field goal by Adam.

At the end of the third quarter, the score was 31–3, Eagles. Ronde turned to the stands and waved to his mom, who beamed back at him and blew him a kiss.

Matt Clayton waved too and gave Ronde a thumbs-up. Ronde smiled and strapped his helmet back on. The Wildcats had just taken possession on their own twenty yard line. "Ronde time," he said to himself as he trotted onto the field.

With a big lead, he reasoned, the Wildcats would have to go to their passing game to try and catch up fast. But if they did, he would make them pay, big-time.

Pulaski tried a long bomb on first down, but it was way overthrown. On second down, they ran a crossing pattern over the middle, but the receiver dropped the pass.

Ronde winced. He knew how badly that kid must feel right now. He'd been there himself. Hadn't they all?

The Wildcats' QB hadn't thrown to Patrick Walsh since the first half, Ronde noticed. That was smart of him, since Ronde was the Eagles' best cornerback and already had an interception and a touchdown.

But sooner or later they would have to try again— and now was the perfect time. On third down and long, needing a first down in the worst way, Ronde guessed that the Wildcats would try a quick square-out pattern.

He dropped back in coverage. But as the ball was snapped, he sprinted right at his man. Sure enough, Walsh wasn't looking at him, but back at the quarterback, waiting for the quick pass.

As soon as he saw Walsh make his move, Ronde cut in front of him and picked the pass right out of the air. In full gallop, he streaked right down the sideline untouched, straight into the end zone!

It was the final, crushing blow for Pulaski. For the rest of the game, the Eagles kept the ball on the ground, running out the clock.

They barely even tried to score. After all, there was no need to humiliate a beaten opponent, and Coach Wheeler made sure they didn't pile on the points in the last five minutes. A 38–3 shellacking of a powerhouse like Pulaski was enough of a statement.

When the final gun sounded, the victorious Eagles ran over to the bleachers to hug their fans and families. They danced up and down in one another's arms.

After hugging his mom and giving Matt Clayton the Eagles' handshake, Ronde happened to notice the reporter for the *Roanoke Reporter* in the back row of the bleachers, scribbling away and shaking his head in amazement.

"Well, why not?" Ronde said to himself. "I'd be shocked too, if I hadn't seen it coming."

CHAPTER THIRTEEN

UNSTOPPABLE

"THAT WAS A DIFFERENT TEAM I SAW OUT THERE tonight," Coach Wheeler said to an excited Eagles team after the game.

The final gun had sounded more than half an hour ago, but only now was everyone back in the locker room. They'd all been doing a lot of celebrating.

It was only a regular season game, Tiki thought, but it meant so much more! It could have been the end of their playoff hopes—but instead, it had brought the Eagles back to life.

Everyone broke out into the team song, clapping their hands and whistling. It seemed like Hidden Valley Junior High was just one big happy family.

It was the first time all season that things were turning out the way Tiki had dreamed they would be. He pinched himself on the arm, hard. No, he wasn't dreaming. This was for real. In fact, it felt like they had all just woken up from a long nightmare!

"You guys really took it to them!" Coach Wheeler told

them. "You brought your A game all night long—and that includes your mental game!"

"You da man, Coach!" Paco shouted, and everybody started chanting, "COACH! COACH! COACH!"

Wheeler raised his hands to quiet them down. "Now you can all see what it takes to beat a powerhouse team like Pulaski. And for tonight, I just want you to enjoy this victory. Because you sure earned it. But one word of warning . . ."

He cast his eagle-eyed gaze around the room, looking each one of them straight in the eye for a moment. "We've got to bring this kind of effort, and do this kind of preparation, every week—that's *every single week*—if we expect to reach our goal this season."

Again, he looked around the room. And this time, when his gaze met Tiki's, he gave his former student a quick little wink.

Tiki knew Coach Wheeler was thanking him for his help that day at Kessler's. He saw the coach wink at Ronde, too.

"We have what some people might call a 'softer schedule' coming up," the coach continued. "So let me warn you right now—if we fall into the trap of looking past teams, and thinking we've got them beat before we step onto the field, I promise you, one of those 'softer' teams is going to rear up and bite us.

"But that's for tomorrow," he finished. "Today, you can give yourselves a great big pat on the back, and score one for our side!"

A huge cheer erupted in the locker room. It echoed off the metal lockers as the stomping of a hundred feet shook the floor.

"COACH, COACH, COACH!"

After Wheeler left the building, the players got showered and changed back into their regular clothes.

Tiki, Ronde, Paco, and Adam walked together out into the parking lot, where Mrs. Barber was waiting by her car to drive them back to the Mews, where they all lived.

"Hey," Adam suddenly said, pointing to the bleachers. "Isn't that? . . ."

"It's Cody," Paco said. "With the guy from the *Roanoke Reporter*!"

Sure enough, Tiki saw the man speaking into a small digital voice recorder. Then he held it up to Cody's face, to record what he said.

"I've got to hear this," Ronde said.

"Man, you are nosy," Tiki said with a laugh.

"Come on with me, Tiki. You know you're curious."

"You are not going over there and snoop on them," Tiki said. "Mom's right over there watching!"

"Okay," Ronde said. "You go—if you get in trouble, just tell them you're me."

"Do it, Tiki!" Paco urged.

"Yeah, man," Adam echoed. "We want to know—and it's important to the team! If he's taking all the credit, and it gets into the paper . . ."

"Don't worry about Mom," Ronde said, seeing Tiki's eyes go to the car. "I'll tell her you're getting interviewed by the paper."

Tiki frowned. "That would be lying, Ronde."

"Not really," Ronde said. "If you work it right, that reporter's bound to ask you a couple of questions too."

Before Tiki could protest, Ronde, Paco, and Adam had already moved off toward Mrs. Barber and the car.

Tiki wandered over toward Cody and the reporter, pretending he didn't notice there was an interview going on.

When he got close enough to hear, he came to a halt, leaning against a lamppost and pretending to fix the zipper on his equipment bag.

"So how does it feel to have a breakthrough performance like the one you had tonight?" the reporter was asking.

Cody smiled. "Well, as far as I'm concerned, the important thing is that the team got a win today."

The reporter nodded. "Yes? And what about your own performance? Seventeen completions on twenty-one passes, three touchdowns, no interceptions or fumbles, seventy-four yards rushing? . . ."

Cody shrugged. "I had good protection, good blocking, my receivers ran great patterns, we all held on to the football, and our coach had a great game plan. I'm just one guy—it takes all fifty of us to play a game like this and win."

The reporter laughed. "You're just being modest."

"Whatever," Cody said. "Just don't write about me being some kind of star, okay? It was a team effort—make sure your article says that."

The reporter put away his pad. "Thanks, Hansen," he said, shaking hands. "And we'll be talking again next week."

Tiki shook his head with a grin. Listening to Cody now, he wouldn't have believed it possible just a few days ago. Cody had gone from being a hotdogging brat who blamed everything that went wrong on somebody else to a real leader who could rally his players behind him.

Cody had changed so much in such a short time! They all had.

Somehow, everything had fallen into place. Coach Wheeler had found a way to get through to Cody. And the Eagles had come back from the brink of disaster.

From here on in, if they stuck to Coach Wheeler's game plan, they would become a legitimate contender for the playoffs, just like everyone thought they would be at the start of the season.

Tiki smiled and blew out a relieved breath. *Coach Wheeler was right,* he thought. *It's all about the mental game!*

FOOTBALL PLAYS

BLITZ
A defensive play. The defensive team rushes the quarterback of the offensive team right after the snap. In this play the defensive team's goal is to sack the quarterback.

BOOTLEG
In this offensive play the quarterback pretends to hand off the football to the running back. Instead, the quarterback runs to the other side of the field so that he can pass or run the ball himself.

CHECK WITH ME
This is an offensive play that is called by the quarterback while the team is in a huddle. The quarterback gives the players two different plays that he wants to run. When they are at the line of scrimmage, the quarterback tells the team which play they are going to do.

FLEA FLICKER
A double reverse play where the quarterback passes the ball to a running back, who passes it back to the quarterback in a double reverse, and then the quarterback passes the football to a receiver.

FREE KICK
At the beginning of each half, and between field goals and touchdowns, this kicking play is used. The kicking team gets to choose how they want to line up behind the football. Meanwhile, the receiving team has to be at least ten yards away from the ball.

HAIL MARY PASS

This is a risky offensive play. The quarterback throws the football with no particular receiver as his target. He hopes that someone on his team will catch it. This play is used when the offensive team is in the end zone.

HOOK AND LADDER

Nickname for "Hook and Lateral." This is a pass play. The receiver catches the football while he is facing the line of scrimmage. Then he laterals the ball to another team member who is already running to the end zone. This is often called a trick play.

LEAD

This is an offensive play. The fullback goes through a bubble in order to block the linebacker. The ball carrier follows him.

MISDIRECTION PLAY

This kind of offensive play fools the defensive team. The play starts to go in one direction and then goes in another instead.

OPTION

In this offensive play the ball carrier gets to choose if he will keep the ball. He can also pass, run, or pitch the football to another teammate.

PLAY-ACTION PASS

The quarterback fakes a handoff to the running back but really turns around to pass the ball. This tricks the opposing team into thinking that the running back is running the ball.

SPINNING FULLBACK

The ball is snapped to a fullback in this offensive play. After the fullback catches the ball, he spins 180° to throw the football to the running back or the quarterback. Sometimes he fakes this and keeps the ball for himself.

STATUE OF LIBERTY PLAY

In this play the ball carrier raises his arm like he's going to pass it. But instead of him throwing the football, another player from his team runs up behind him to grab the ball. This is a fake pass play.

SWEEP

This is an offensive play. The quarterback pitches or hands the football to the running back. Then the running back can turn the ball upfield more easily.

SWINGING GATE

A trick play. The offensive team lines up on one side of the field, leaving the running back and the quarterback unguarded on the other side. The defense is then forced to create a defensive play on the spot.

TRAP PLAY

This play uses a block that can fool the defensive team. At the same time as the snap, an offensive lineman pulls out of the line. This tricks his defensive target into thinking that no one will block him. The lineman really traps the defensive player to make a hole for one of his teammates to get through.

TRICK PLAY

This means an unusual play. Since trick plays aren't expected by the opposing team, they are usually successful. They can't be used too often, however, or they won't work as well.